There is a Garan

who lies in the Cavern of the Sleepers and whose story Thrala has told me. But before him—long before—there were others.

For when I questioned the Daughter of the Ancient Ones, she took me into one of the curious rooms where are mirrors of seeing embedded in tables. There she seated herself, drawing me down beside her.

"What we did, we two, on the vanished world of Krand, has lain between us for long—long. It being gone at last, I half fear to summon it again. We have paid the price, three times over have we paid it. Once in Yu-Lac and twice in the Caverns. And now it pleases me to look again upon the most splendid act I have ever witnessed.

"Behold, my lord."

She raised her slender hands above the mirror. It misted. . . .

GARAN
THE
ETERNAL

Andre Norton

DAW BOOKS, INC.
DONALD A. WOLLHEIM, PUBLISHER

1633 Broadway, New York, NY 10019

DAW Book Collectors' Number 45

FIRST DAW PRINTING: MARCH 1973

6 7 8 9 10

PRINTED IN THE U.S.A.

Contents

PART ONE

1

Through the Blue Haze

Six months and three days after the Peace of Shanghai was signed and the Great War of 1985-88 declared at an end by an exhausted world, a young man huddled on a park bench in New York, staring forlornly at the gravel beneath his badly worn shoes. He had been trained to fill the pilot's seat in the control cabin of a fighter plane and for nothing else. The search for a niche in civilian life had cost him both health and ambition.

A newcomer dropped down on the other end of the bench. The flyer studied him bitterly. *He* had decent shoes, a warm coat, and that air of satisfaction with the world which is the result of economic security. Although he was well into middle age, the man had a compact grace of movement and an air of alertness.

"Aren't you Captain Garin Featherstone?"

Startled, the flier nodded assent. Two years before he, Captain Garin Featherstone of the United Democratic Forces, had led a perilous bombing raid into the wastelands of Asia to wipe out a vast expeditionary army secretly gathering there. It had been a spectacular affair and had brought the survivors some fleeting fame.

From a plump billfold the newcomer drew a clipping and waved it toward his seat mate.

"You're the man I've been looking for"—the stranger refolded the clipping—"a pilot with courage, initiative, and brains. The man who led that raid is worth investing in."

"What's the proposition?" asked Featherstone wearily. He no longer believed in luck.

"I'm Gregory Farson," the other returned as if that should answer the question.

"The Antarctic man?"

"Just so. As you have probably heard, I was stopped on the eve of my last expedition by the sudden spread of the war to this country. Now I am preparing to sail south again."

"But I don't see—"

"How you can help me? Very simple, Captain Featherstone. I need pilots. Unfortunately the war has disposed of most of them. I'm lucky to contact one such as yourself—"

And it was as simple as that. But Garin didn't really believe it until they touched the glacial shores of the polar continent some months later. As they brought ashore the three large planes he began to wonder at the driving motive behind Farson's vague plans.

When the supply ship sailed, not to return for a year, Farson called them together. Three of the company were pilots, all war veterans, and two were engineers who spent most of their waking hours engrossed in the maps Farson produced.

"Tomorrow"—the leader glanced from face to

face—"we start inland. Here—" On a map spread before him he indicated a line marked in purple.

"Ten years ago I was a member of the Verdane expedition. Once, when flying due south, our plane was caught by some freakish air current and drawn off its course. When we were totally off our map, we saw in the distance a thick bluish haze. It seemed to rise in a straight line from the ice plain to the sky. Unfortunately our fuel was low and we dared not risk a closer investigation. So we fought our way back to the base.

"Verdane, however, had little interest in our report and we did not investigate it. Three years ago that Kattack expedition, hunting oil deposits by order of the Dictator, reported seeing the same haze. This time we are going to explore it!"

"Why," Garin asked curiously, "are you so eager to penetrate this haze?"

Farson hesitated before answering. "It has often been suggested that beneath the ice sheeting of this continent there is hidden mineral wealth. I believe the haze is caused by some form of volcanic activity, and perhaps a break in the crust."

Garin frowned at the map. He wasn't so sure about that explanation, but Farson was paying the bills. He shrugged away his uneasiness. Much could be forgiven a man who allowed one to eat regularly again.

Four days later they set out. Helmly, one of the engineers, Rawlson, a pilot, and Farson occupied the first plane. The other engineer and pilot were both in the second and Garin, with the extra supplies, was alone in the third.

He was content to be alone as they took off across the blue-white waste. His ship, because of the load, was loggy, so he did not attempt to follow the other two into the higher lane. They were in communication by radio and Garin, as he snapped on his earphones, remembered something Farson had said that morning.

"The haze affects radio. On our trip near it the static was very bad. Almost"—with a laugh—"like speech in some foreign tongue."

As they roared over the ice Garin wondered if it might have been speech—from, perhaps, a secret enemy expedition, such as the Kattack one.

In his sealed cabin he did not feel the bite of the frost and the ship rode smoothly. With a little sigh of content he settled back against the cushions, keeping to the course set by the planes ahead and above him.

About an hour after they left the base, Garin caught sight of a dark shadow far ahead. At the same time Farson's voice chattered on his radio.

"That's it. Set course straight ahead."

The shadow grew until it became a wall of purple-blue from earth to sky. The first plane was quite close to it, diving down into the vapor. Suddenly the ship rocked violently and swung earthward as if out of control. Then it straightened and turned back. Garin could hear Farson demanding to know what was the matter. But from the first plane there was no reply.

As Farson's plane kept going Garin throttled down. The actions of the first ship indicated trouble. What if that haze were a toxic gas?

"Close up, Featherstone!" barked Farson suddenly.

He obediently drew ahead until they flew wing to wing. The haze was just before them and now Garin could see movement in it, oily, impenetrable billows. The motors bit into it. There was clammy, foggy moisture on the windows.

Abruptly Garin sensed that he was no longer alone. Somewhere in the empty cabin behind him was another intelligence, a measuring power. He fought furiously against it—against the very idea of it. But, after a long terrifying moment while it seemed to study him, it took control. His hands and feet still manipulated the ship, but the alien controlled him.

The ship hurtled on through the thickening mist. He lost sight of Farson's plane. And, though he was still fighting against the will which overrode his, his struggles grew weaker. Then came the order to dive into the dark heart of the purple mists.

Down they whirled. Once, as the haze opened, Garin caught a glimpse of tortured gray rock seamed with yellow. Farson had been right: here the ice crust was broken.

Down and down. If his instruments were correct the plane was below sea level now. The haze thinned and was gone. Below spread a plain cloaked in vivid green. Here and there reared clumps of what might be trees. He saw, too, the waters of a yellow stream.

But there was something terrifyingly alien about that landscape. Even as he circled above it, Garin strove to break the grip of the will that had brought him here. There came a cackle of sound in his earphones and at that moment the Presence withdrew.

The nose of the plane went up in obedience to his own desire. Frantically he climbed away from the green land. Again the haze absorbed him. He watched the moisture bead on the windows. Another hundred feet or so and he would be free of it—and that unbelievable world beneath.

Then, with an ominous sputter, the port engine conked out. The plane lurched and slipped into a dive. Down it whirled again into the steady light of the green land.

Trees came out of the ground, huge fern-like plants

with crimson scaled trunks. Toward a clump of these the plane swooped.

Frantically Garin fought the controls. The ship steadied, the dive became a fast glide. He looked for an open space to land. Then he felt the landing gear scrape some surface. Directly ahead loomed one of the fern trees. The plane sped toward the long fronds. There came a ripping crash, the splintering of metal and wood. The scarlet cloud gathering before Garin's eyes turned black.

Garin returned to consciousness through a red mist of pain. He was pinned in the crumpled mass of metal which had once been the cabin. Through a rent in the wall close to his head thrust a long spike of green, shredded leaves still clinging to it. He lay and watched it, not daring to move lest the pain prove more than he could bear.

It was then that he heard the pattering sound outside. It seemed as if soft hands were pushing and pulling at the wreck. The tree branch shook and a portion of the cabin wall dropped away with a clang.

Garin turned his head slowly. Through the aperture was clambering a goblin-like figure.

It stood about five feet tall, and it walked upon its hind legs in human fashion, but the legs were short and stumpy, ending in feet with five toes of equal length. Slender, shapely arms possessed small hands with only four digits. The creature had a high, well-rounded forehead but no chin, the face being distinctly lizard-like in contour. The skin was a dull black with a velvety surface. About its loins it wore a short kilt of metallic cloth, the garment being supported by a jeweled belt of exquisite workmanship.

For a long moment the apparition eyed Garin. And it was those golden eyes, fixed unwinkingly on his,

which banished the flier's fear. There was nothing
but great pity in their depths.

The lizard-man stooped and brushed the sweat-
dampened hair from Garin's forehead. Then he fingered the bonds of metal which held the flier, as if
estimating their strength. Having done so, he turned
to the opening and apparently gave an order, returning again to squat by Garin.

Two more of his kind appeared, to tear away the
ruins of the cabin. Though they were very careful,
Garin lost consciousness before they had him free.

When Garin again became aware of his surroundings, he discovered he was on a litter swung between
two clumsy beasts which might have been small
elephants, except that they lacked trunks and possessed four tusks each.

They crossed the plain to the towering mouth of a
huge cavern where the litter was taken up by four of
the lizard-folk. Garin lay staring up at the roof of the
cavern. In the black stone had been carved fronds and
flowers in bewildering profusion. Shining motes, giving off faint light, sifted through the air. At times as
they advanced these gathered in clusters and the light
grew brighter.

Midway down a long corridor the bearers halted
while their leader pulled upon a knob on the wall. An
oval door swung back and the party passed through.

They came into a round room, the walls of which
had been fashioned of creamy quartz veined with
violet. At the highest point in the ceiling a large
globe of the motes hung, furnishing soft light below.

Two lizard-men, clad in long robes, conferred with
the leader of the flier's party before coming to stand
over Garin. One of the robed ones shook his head at
the sight of the flier's twisted body and waved the
litter on into an inner chamber.

Here the walls were dull blue and in the exact center was a long block of quartz. The litter was put down atop this and the bearers disappeared. With sharp knives the robed men cut away furs and leather to expose Garin's broken body.

They lifted him to the quartz table and there made him fast with metal bonds. Then one of them went to the wall and pulled a gleaming rod. An eerie blue light shot out from the dome of the roof to beat upon the helpless Garin. He felt a tingling through every muscle and joint, a prickling sensation in his skin, and soon his pain vanished as if it had never been.

The light flashed off and the three lizard-men gathered around him. He was wrapped in a soft robe and carried to another room. This, too, was circular, shaped like the half of a giant bubble. The floor sloped toward the center where there was a depression filled with cushions. There they laid Garin. At the top of the bubble, a pinkish cloud formed. He watched it drowsily until he fell asleep.

Something warm stirred against his bare shoulder. He opened his eyes, for a moment unable to remember where he was. Then there was a plucking at the robe twisted about him and he looked down.

If the lizard-folk had been goblin-like in their grotesqueness this visitor was elfin. It was about three feet high, its monkey-like body completely covered with silky white hair. The tiny hands were human in shape and hairless, but its feet were much like a cat's paws. From either side of the small round head branched large fan-shaped ears. The face was furred and boasted stiff cat whiskers on the upper lip. These *Anas,* as Garin learned later, were happy little creatures, each one choosing some mistress or master among the Folk, as this one had come to him. They were content to follow their big protector, speechless with delight at trifling gifts. Loyal and brave, they could do simple tasks or carry written messages for their chosen friend, and they remained with him until death. They were neither beast nor human, but rumored to be the result of some experiment carried out eons ago by the Ancient Ones.

After patting Garin's shoulder the Ana touched the flier's hair wonderingly, comparing the bronze lengths with its own white fur. Since the Folk were hairless, hair was a strange sight in the Caverns. With a contented purr, the Ana rubbed its head against his hand.

With a sudden click a door in the wall opened. The Ana got to its feet and ran to greet the newcomers. The Chieftain of the Folk, he who had first found Garin, entered, followed by several of his fellows.

The flier sat up. Not only was the pain gone but he felt stronger and younger than he had for weary months. Exultingly he stretched wide his arms and grinned at the lizard-being who murmured happily in return.

Lizard-men busied themselves about Garin, girding on him the short kilt and jewel-set belt, apparently the only clothing being worn within the Caverns. When they were finished, the Chieftain took his hand and drew him to the door.

They traversed a hallway whose walls were carved and inlaid with glittering stones and metal work, coming, at last, into a huge cavern, the outer walls of which were hidden by shadows. On a dais stood three tall thrones and Garin was conducted to the foot of these.

The highest throne was of rose crystal. On its right was one of green jade, worn smooth by centuries of time. The one at the left was carved of a single block of jet. The rose throne and the jet one were unoccupied, but in the seat of jade reposed one of the Folk. He was taller than his fellows and in his eyes, as he stared at Garin, was wisdom—and a brooding sadness.

"It is well!" The words resounded in the flier's head. "We have chosen wisely. This youth is fit to mate with the Daughter. But he will be tried, as fire tries metal. He must win the Daughter forth and strive with Kepta—"

A hissing murmur echoed through the hall. Garin guessed that hundreds of the Folk must be gathered there.

"Urg!" the being on the throne commanded.

"Take this youth and instruct him. And then I will speak with him again. For"—sadness colored the words now—"we would have the rose throne filled again and the black one blasted into dust. Time moves swiftly."

The Chieftain led a wondering Garin away.

2
Garin Learns of the Black Ones

Urg brought the flier into one of the bubble-shaped rooms which contained a low, cushioned bench facing a metal screen—and here they seated themselves.

What followed was a language lesson. On the screen appeared objects which Urg would name, to have his sibilant uttering repeated by Garin. As the American later learned, the ray treatment he had undergone had quickened his mental powers and in an incredibly short time he had a working vocabulary.

Judging by the pictures the lizard folk were the rulers of the crater world, although there were other forms of life there. The elephant-like *Tand* was a beast of burden, the squirrel-like *Eron* lived underground and carried on a crude agriculture in small clearings, coming shyly twice a year to exchange grain for a liquid rubber produced by the Folk.

Then there was the *Gibi*, a monstrous bee, also friendly to the lizard people. It supplied the cavern dwellers with wax and in return the Folk gave the

Gibi colonies shelter during the unhealthful times of the Great Mists.

Highly civilized were the Folk. They did no work by hand, except the finer kinds of jewel settings and carving. Machines wove their metal cloth, machines prepared their food, harvested their fields, hollowed out new dwellings.

Freed from manual labor they had turned to acquiring knowledge. Urg projected pictures on the screen of vast laboratories and great libraries of scientific lore. But all they knew in the beginning, they had learned from the Ancient Ones, a race unlike themselves, which had preceded them in sovereignty over *Tav*. Even the Folk themselves were the result of constant forced evolution and experimentation carried on by these Ancient Ones.

All this wisdom was guarded most carefully; but against what or whom, Urg could not tell, although he insisted the danger was very real. There was something written within the blue wall of the crater which disputed the Folk's rule.

As Garin tried to probe further a gong sounded. Urg arose.

"It is the hour of eating," he announced. "Let us go."

They came to a large room where a heavy table of white stone stretched along three walls, benches before it. Urg seated himself and pressed a knob on the table, motioning Garin to do likewise. The wall facing them opened and two trays slid out. There was a platter of hot meat covered with rich sauce, a stone bowl of grain porridge and a cluster of fruit, still fastened to a leafy branch. This the Ana eyed so wistfully that Garin gave it to the creature.

The Folk ate silently and arose quietly when they had finished, their trays vanishing back through the wall. Garin noticed only males in the room and recalled that he had, as yet, seen no females among the Folk. He ventured a question.

Urg chuckled. "So you think there are no women in the Caverns? Well, we shall go to the Hall of Women that you may see."

To the Hall of Women they went. It was breathtaking in its richness, stones worth a nation's ransom sparkling from its domed roof and painted walls. Here were the matrons and maidens of the Folk, their black forms veiled in robes of silver net, each cross strand of which was set with a tiny gem, so that they appeared to be wrapped in glittering scales.

There were not many of them—a hundred perhaps. And a few led by the hand smaller editions of themselves who stared at Garin with round yellow eyes and chewed black fingertips shyly.

The women were entrusted with the finest jewel work, and with pride they showed the stranger their handiwork. At the far end of the hall was a wondrous thing in the making. One of the silver nets which were the foundations of their robes was fastened there and three of the women were putting small rose jewels into each microscopic setting. Here and there they had varied the pattern with tiny emeralds or flaming opals so that the finished portion was a rainbow.

One of the workers smoothed the robe and glanced up at Garin, a gentle teasing in her voice as she explained:

"This is for the Daughter when she comes to her throne."

The Daughter! What had the Lord of the Folk said? "This youth is fit to mate with the Daughter." But Urg had said that the Ancient Ones had gone from Tav.

"Who is the Daughter?" he demanded.

"Thrala of the Light."

"Where is she?"

The woman shivered and there was fear in her eyes. "Thrala lies in the Caves of Darkness."

"The Caves of Darkness!" Did she mean Thrala was dead? Was he, Garin Featherstone, to be the victim of some rite of sacrifice which was designed to unite him with the dead?

Urg touched his arm. "Not so. Thrala has not yet entered the Place of Ancestors."

"You know my thoughts?"

Urg laughed. "Thoughts are easy to read. Thrala lives. Sera served the Daughter as handmaiden while she was yet among us. Sera, please show us Thrala as she was."

The woman crossed to a wall where there was a mirror such as Urg had used for Garin's language lesson. She gazed into it and then beckoned the flier to stand beside her.

The mirror misted and then he was looking, as if through a window, into a room with walls and ceiling of rose quartz. On the floor were thick rugs of silver rose. And a great heap of cushions made a low couch in the center.

"The inner chamber of the Daughter," Sera announced.

A circular panel in the wall opened and a woman slipped through. She was very young, little more than a girl. There were happy curves in her full crimson lips, joyous lights in her violet eyes. Her shape was human, but her beauty was unearthly. Delicate colors seemed to play faintly upon her pearl white skin, reminding Garin of mother-of-pearl with its lights and shadows. Blue-black hair seemed to veil her as a cloud, reaching below her knees. Her robe of silver net was girdled about her waist by rose-shaded jewels.

"That was Thrala before the Black Ones took her," said Sera.

Urg laughed at Garin's cry of disappointment as the picture vanished.

"What care you for shadows when the Daughter herself waits for you? You have but to bring her from the Caves of Darkness. . . ."

"Where are these Caves—" Garin's question was interrupted by the pealing of the Cavern gong.

Sera cried out: "The Black Ones!"

Urg shrugged. "When they spared not the Ancient Ones how could we hope to escape? Come, we must go to the Hall of Thrones."

Before the jade throne of the Lord of the Folk stood a small group of the lizard-men beside two litters. As Garin entered the Lord spoke.

"Let the outlander come hither that he may see the work of the Black Ones."

Garin advanced unwillingly, coming to stand by those struggling things which gasped their message between moans and screams of agony. They were men of the Folk but their black skins were green with rot.

The Lord leaned forward on his throne. "It is well," he said. "You may depart."

As if obeying his command, the tortured things let go of the life to which they had clung and were still.

"Look upon the work of the Black Ones," the ruler said to Garin. "Jiv and Betv were captured while on a mission to the Gibi of the Cliff. It seems that the Black Ones needed material for their laboratories. They seek even to give the Daughter to their workers of horror!"

A terrible cry of hatred arose from the hall, and Garin's jaw set. To give that fair vision he had just seen to such a death as this—!

"Jiv and Betv were imprisoned close to the Daughter and they heard the threats of Kepta. Our brothers, stricken with foul disease, were sent forth to carry the plague to us, but they swam through the pool of boiling mud. They have died but the evil died with them. And I think that while we breed such as they, the Black Ones shall not rest easy. Listen, now, outlander, to the story of the Black Ones and the Caves of Darkness, of how the Ancient Ones brought the Folk up from the slime of a long dried sea and made them great, and of how the Ancient Ones at last went down to their destruction.

"In the days before the lands of the outer world were born of the sea, before even the Land of the Sun (Mu) and the Land of the Sea (Atlantis) arose from molten rock and sand, there was land here in the far south. A sere land of rock and plains and swamps where slimy life mated, lived, and died.

"Then came the Ancient Ones from beyond the stars. Their race was already older than this earth. Their wise men had watched its birth-rending from the sun. And when their world perished, taking most of their blood into nothingness, a handful fled to the new world.

"But when they climbed from their spaceship it was into hell. For they had gained, in place of their loved home, bare rock and stinking slime.

"They blasted out this Tav and entered into it with the treasures of their starships and also certain living creatures captured in the swamps. From these, they produced the Folk, the Gibi, the Tand, and the land-tending Eron.

"Among these, the Folk were eager for wisdom

and climbed high. But still the learning of the Ancient Ones remained beyond their grasp.

"During the eons when the Ancient Ones dwelt within their protecting wall of haze the outer world changed. Cold came to the north and south; the Land of the Sun and the Land of the Sea arose to bear the foot of true man. On their mirrors of seeing the Ancient Ones watched man-life spread across the world. They had the power of prolonging life, but still the race was dying. From without must come new blood. So certain men were summoned from the Land of the Sun. Then the race flourished for a space.

"The Ancient Ones decided to leave Tav for the outer world. But the sea swallowed the Land of the Sun. Again in the time of the Land of the Sea the stock within Tav was replenished and the Ancient Ones prepared for exodus; again the sea cheated them.

"Those men left in the outer world reverted to savagery. Since the Ancient Ones would not mingle their blood with that of almost beasts, they built the haze wall stronger and remained. But a handful of them were attracted by the forbidden, and secretly summoned the beast men. Of that monstrous mating came the Black Ones. They live but for the evil they may do, and the power which they acquired is debased and used to forward cruelty.

"At first their sin was not discovered. When it was, the others would have slain the offspring but for the law which forbids them to kill. They must use their power for good or it departs from them. So they drove the Black Ones to the southern end of Tav and gave them the Caves of Darkness. Never were the Black Ones to come north of the River of Gold—nor were the Ancient Ones to go south of it.

"For perhaps two thousand years the Black Ones kept the law. But they worked, building powers of destruction. While matters rested thus, the Ancient Ones searched the world, seeking men by whom they could renew the race. Once there came men from an island far to the north. Six lived to penetrate the mists and take wives among the Daughters. Again, they called the yellow-haired men of another breed, great sea rovers.

"But the Black Ones called too. As the Ancient Ones searched for the best, the Black Ones brought in great workers of evil. And, at last, they succeeded in shutting off the channels of sending thought so that the Ancient Ones could call no more.

"Then did the Black Ones cross the River of Gold and enter the land of the Ancient Ones. Thran, Dweller in the Light and Lord of the Caverns, summoned the Folk to him.

" 'There will come one to aid you,' he told us. 'Try the summoning again after the Black Ones have seemed to win. Thrala, daughter of the Light, will not enter into the Room of Pleasant Death with the rest of the women, but will give herself into the hands of the Black Ones that they may think themselves truly victorious. You of the Folk withdraw into the Place of Reptiles until the Black Ones are gone. Nor will all of the Ancient Ones perish—more will be saved, but the manner of their preservation I dare not tell. When the sun-haired youth comes from the outer world, send him into the Caves of Darkness to rescue Thrala and put an end to evil.'

"And then the Lady Thrala arose and said softly, 'As the Lord Thran has said, so let it be. I shall deliver myself into the hands of the Black Ones that their doom may come upon them.'

"Lord Thran smiled upon her as he said: 'So will

happiness be your portion. After the Great Mists, does not light come again?''

"The women of the Ancient Ones then took their leave and passed into the Room of Pleasant Death while the men made ready for battle with the Black Ones. For three days they fought, but a new weapon of the Black Ones won the day, and the chief of the Black Ones set up this throne of jet as proof of his power. Since, however, the Black Ones were not happy in the Caverns, longing for the darkness of their caves, they soon withdrew and we, the Folk, came forth again.

"But now the time has come when the dark ones will sacrifice the Daughter to their evil. If you can win her free, outlander, they shall perish as if they had not been.''

"What of the Ancient Ones?" asked Garin. "Those others Thran said would be saved?"

"Of those we know nothing save that when we bore the bodies of the fallen to the Place of Ancestors there were some missing. That you may see the truth of this story, Urg will take you to the gallery above the Room of Pleasant Death and you may look upon those who sleep there.''

Urg guiding, Garin climbed a steep ramp leading from the Hall of Thrones. This led to a narrow balcony, one side of which was clear crystal. Urg pointed down.

They were above a long room whose walls were tinted jade green. On the polished floor were scattered piles of cushions. Each was occupied by a sleeping woman and several of these clasped a child in their arms. Their long hair rippled to the floor, their curved lashes made dark shadows on pale faces.

"But they are sleeping!" protested Garin.

Urg shook his head. "It is the sleep of death.

Twice each ten hours vapors rise from the floor. Those breathing them do not wake again, and if they are undisturbed they will lie thus for a thousand years. Look there—"

He pointed to the closed double doors of the room. There lay the first men of the Ancient Ones that Garin had seen. They, too, seemed but asleep, their handsome heads pillowed on their arms.

"Thran ordered those who remained after the last battle in the Hall of Thrones to enter the Room of Pleasant Death that the Black Ones might not torture them for their beastly pleasures. Thran himself remained behind to close the door, and so died."

There were no aged among the sleepers. None of the men seemed to count more than thirty years and many of them appeared younger. Garin remarked upon this.

"The Ancient Ones appeared thus until the day of their death, though many lived twice a hundred years. The ray kept them so. Even we of the Folk can hold back age. But come now, our Lord Trar would speak with you again."

Again Garin stood before the jade throne of Trar and heard the stirring of the multitude of the Folk in the shadows. Trar was turning a small rod of glittering, greenish metal around in his soft hands.

"Listen well, outlander," he began, "for little time remains to us. Within seven days the Great Mists will be upon us. Then no living thing may venture forth from shelter and escape death. And before that time Thrala must be out of the Caves. This rod will be your weapon; the Black Ones have not its secret. Watch."

Two of the Folk dragged an ingot of metal before him. He touched it with the rod. Great flakes of rust appeared, to spread across the entire surface. It crumpled away and one of the Folk trod upon the pile of dust where it had been.

"Thrala lies in the heart of the Caves but Kepta's men have grown careless with the years. Enter boldly and trust to fortune. They know nothing of your coming or of Thran's words concerning you."

Urg stood forward and held out his hands in appeal.

"What is it, Urg?"

"Lord, I would like to go with the outlander. He knows nothing of the Forest of the Morgels or of the Pool of Mud. It is easy to go astray in the woodland—"

Trar shook his head. "That may not be. He must go alone, even as Thran said."

The Ana, which had followed in Garin's shadow all day, whistled shrilly and stood on tiptoe to tug at his hand.

Trar smiled. "That one may go; its eyes may serve you well. Urg will guide you to the outer portal of the Place of Ancestors and set you upon the road to the Caves. Farewell, outlander, and may the spirits of the Ancient Ones be with you."

Garin bowed to the ruler of the Folk and turned to follow Urg. Near the door stood a small group of women. Sera pressed forward from them, holding out a small bag.

"Outlander," she said hurriedly, "when you look upon the Daughter speak to her of Sera, for I have awaited her many years."

He smiled. "That I will."

"If you remember, outlander. I am a great lady among the Folk and have my share of suitors, yet I think I could envy the Daughter. Nay, I shall not explain that." She laughed mockingly. "You will understand in due time. Here is a packet of food.

Now go swiftly that we may have you among us
again before the Mists.''

So a woman's farewell sped them on their way.
Urg chose a ramp that led downward. At its foot was
a niche in the rock, above which a rose light burned
dimly. Urg reached within the hollow and drew out a
pair of high buskins which he aided Garin to lace on.
They were a good fit, having been fashioned for a
man of the Ancient Ones.

The passage before them was narrow and crooked.
There was a thick carpet of dust underfoot, patterned
by the prints of the Folk. They rounded a corner and
a tall door loomed out of the gloom. Urg pressed the
surface; there was a click and the stone rolled back.

''This is the Place of the Ancestors,'' he announced
as he stepped within.

They were at the entrance of a colossal hall whose
domed roof disappeared into shadows. Thick pillars
of gleaming crystal divided it into aisles all leading
inward to a raised dais of oval shape. Filling the
aisles were couches and each soft nest held its sleeper.
Near to the door lay the men and women of the Folk,
but closer to the dais were the Ancient Ones. Here
and there a couch bore an inscription. A son of
pre-Norman Ireland. Urg traced with a crooked finger
the archaic lettering carved upon the stone base of the
couch.

''Lovers in the Light sleep sweetly. The Light
returns on the appointed day.''

''Who lies there?'' Garin motioned to the dais.

''The first Ancient Ones. Come, look upon those
who made this Tav.''

On the dais the couches were arranged in two
rows and between them, in their center, was a single
couch raised above the others. Fifty men and women
lay as if but resting for the hour, smiles on their

peaceful faces but weary shadows beneath their eyes. There was an inhuman quality about them which was lacking in their descendants.

Urg advanced to the high couch and beckoned Garin to join him. A man and a woman lay there; upon the man's shoulder was pillowed the woman's drooping head. Urg stopped beside them.

"See, outlander, here was one who was called from your world. Marena of the House of Light looked with favor upon him and their days of happiness were many."

The man on the couch had red-gold hair and on his upper arm was a heavy band of gold whose mate Garin had once seen in a man's breast. There was that in their faces which made Garin turn away. He felt as if he had intruded roughly where no man should go.

"Here lies Thran, Son of Light, first Lord of the Caverns, and his lady Thrala, Dweller in the Light. So have they lain a thousand years, and so will they lie until this planet rots to dust beneath them. They led the Folk out of the slime and made Tav. Such as they we shall never see again."

They passed silently down the aisles of the dead. Once Garin caught sight of another fair-haired man, perhaps another outlander, since the Ancient Ones were all dark-haired. Urg paused once more before they left the hall. He stood by the couch of a man, wrapped in a long robe, whose face was ravaged with marks of agony.

Urg spoke a single name: "Thran."

So this was the last Lord of the Caverns. Garin leaned closer to study the dead face but Urg seemed to have lost his patience. He hurried his charge on to a paneled door.

"This is the southern portal of the Caverns," he

explained. "Trust to the Ana to guide you and beware of the boiling mud. Should the morgels scent you, kill quickly; they are the servants of the Black Ones. May fortune favor you, outlander."

The door was open and Garin looked out upon Tav. The soft blue light was as strong as it had been when he had first seen it. With the Ana perched on his shoulder and the green rod and the bag of food in his hands, he stepped out onto the moss sod.

Urg raised his hand in salute and the door clicked into place. Garin stood alone, pledged to bring the Daughter out of the Caves of Darkness.

3

Into the Caves of Darkness

There is no light nor day in Tav since the blue light is steady. But the Folk divide their time by artificial means. However Garin, being newly come from the rays of healing, felt no fatigue. As he hesitated the Ana chattered and pointed confidently ahead.

Before them was a dense wood of fern trees. It was quiet in the forest as Garin made his way into its gloom and for the first time he noted a peculiarity of Tav. There were no birds.

The portion of the woodland they had to traverse was but a spur of the forest to the west. After an hour of travel they came out upon the bank of a sluggish river. The turbid waters of the stream were a dull saffron color. Garin decided that it must be the River of Gold, boundary of the lands of the Black Ones.

He rounded a bend and came upon a bridge, so old that time itself had worn its stone angles into curves. The bridge gave onto a wide plain where tall grass grew sere and yellow. To the left was a hissing and bubbling, and a huge vaporous mass arose in the air.

Garin choked in a wind, thick with chemicals, which blew from it. He smelled and tasted the sulphur-tainted air all across the plain.

And he was glad to plunge into a small fern grove which half concealed a spring. There he bathed his head and arms while the Ana pulled open the food bag Sera had given them.

Together they ate the cakes of grain and dried fruit. When they were done the Ana tugged at Garin's hand and pointed on.

Cautiously Garin wormed his way through the thick underbrush until, at last, he looked out into a clearing and saw at its edge the entrance of the Black Ones' Caves. Two tall pillars, carved into the likeness of foul monsters, guarded a rough-edged hole. A fine greenish mist whirled and danced in its mouth.

Garin studied the entrance. There was no life to be seen. He gripped the destroying rod and inched forward. Before the green mist he braced himself and then stepped within.

The green mist enveloped Garin. He drew into his lungs hot moist air faintly tinged with a scent of sickly sweetness as from some hidden corruption. Green motes in the air gave forth little light and seemed to cling to the intruder.

With the Ana pattering before him, he started down a steep ramp, the soft soles of his buskins making no sound. At regular intervals along the wall, niches held small statues. And about each perverted figure was a crown of green motes.

The Ana stopped, its large ears outspread as if to catch the faintest murmur of sound. From somewhere under the earth came the howls of a maddened dog. The Ana shivered, creeping closer to Garin.

Down led the ramp, growing narrower and steeper. And louder sounded the insane, coughing howls of

the dog. Then the passage was abruptly barred by a
grill of black stone. Garin peered through its bars at a
flight of stairs leading down into a pit. From the pit
arose snarling laughter.

Padding back and forth were things which might
have been conceived by demons. They were sleek,
rat-like creatures, hairless, and large as ponies. Red
saliva dripped from the corners of their sharp jaws.
But in the eyes, which they raised now and then
toward the grill, there was intelligence. These were
the morgels, watchdogs and slaves of the Black Ones.

From a second pair of stairs directly across the pit
arose a moaning call. A door opened and two men
came down the steps. The morgels surged forward,
but fell back when whips were cracked over their
heads.

The masters of the morgels were human in appearance. Black loincloths were twisted about them and
long, wing-shaped cloaks hung from their shoulders.
On their heads, completely masking their hair, were
cloth caps which bore ragged crests not unlike cocks-
combs. As far as Garin could see they were unarmed
except for their whips.

A second party was coming down the steps. Between two of the Black Ones struggled a prisoner. He
made a desperate and hopeless fight of it, but they
dragged him to the edge of the pit before they stopped.
The morgels, intent upon their promised prey, crouched
beneath them.

Five steps above were two figures to whom the
guards looked for instructions. One was a man of their
race, of slender, handsome body and evil, coldly
patrician face. His hand rested possessively upon the
arm of his companion.

It was Thrala who stood beside him, her head
proudly erect. The curves of laughter were gone from

her lips; there was only sorrow and resignation to be seen there now. But her spirit burned like a white flame in her eyes.

"Look!" her warder ordered. "Does not Kepta keep his promises? Shall we give Dandtan into the jaws of our slaves, or will you take back certain words of yours, Lady Thrala?"

The prisoner answered for her: "Kepta, son of vileness, Thrala is not for you. Remember, Beloved One"—he spoke directly to the Daughter—"the day of deliverance is at hand!"

Garin felt a sudden strange emptiness at the ease with which the prisoner had called Thrala "beloved."

"I await Thrala's answer," Kepta demanded. And her answer he got.

"Beast among beasts, you may send Dandtan to his death, you may heap all manner of insults and evil upon me, but still I say the Daughter is not for your touch. Rather will I cut the line of life with my own hands, taking upon me the punishment of the Elder Ones." She lowered her gaze to the prisoner. "To you, Dandtan, I say farewell. We shall meet again beyond the Curtain of Time." She held out her hands to him.

"Thrala, dear one—!" One of his guards slapped a hand over the prisoner's mouth, putting an end to his words.

But now Thrala was looking beyond him, straight at the grill which sheltered Garin. Kepta pulled at her arm to gain her attention. "Watch! Thus do my enemies die. To the pit with him!"

The guards forced their prisoner toward the edge of the pit and the morgels crept closer, their eyes fixed upon that young, writhing body. Garin knew that he must take no hand in the game. The Ana was tugging him to the right and there was an open

archway leading to a balcony running around the side
of the pit.

Those below were too entranced by the coming
sport to notice the invader. But Thrala glanced up
and Garin thought that she sighted him. Something in
her attitude attracted Kepta; he too looked up. For a
moment he stared in stark amazement, and then he
thrust the Daughter through the door behind him.

"Ho, outlander! Welcome to the Caves. So the
Folk have meddled—"

"Greeting, Kepta." Garin himself was surprised at
the words which fell so easily from his tongue. "I
have come as was promised, to remain until the
Black Throne is no more."

"Not even the morgels boast before their prey lies
limp in their jaws," flashed Kepta. "What manner of
beast are you?"

"A clean beast, Kepta, which you are not. Bid
your two-legged morgels loose the youth, lest I grow
impatient." He swung the green rod into view.

Kepta's eyes narrowed but his smile did not fade.
"I have heard of old that the Ancient Ones do not
destroy—"

"As an outlander I am not bound by their limits,"
retorted Garin, "as you will learn if you do not call
off your stinking pack."

The master of the Caves laughed. "You are as the
Tand, a fool without a brain. Never shall you see the
Caverns again—"

"You have a choice, Kepta. Make it quickly."

The Black Chief seemed to consider. Then he
waved to his men. "Release him," he ordered. "Outlander, you are braver than I thought. We might
bargain—"

"Thrala goes forth from the Caves and the black
throne is dust, those are the terms of the Caverns."

"And if we do not accept?"

"Then Thrala goes forth, the throne is dust, and Tav shall have a day of judging such as it has never had before."

"You challenge me?"

Again words which seemed to have their origin elsewhere came to Garin. "As in Yu-Lac, I shall take—"

Before Kepta could reply there was trouble in the pit. Dandtan, freed by his guards, was crossing the floor in running leaps with the morgels in hot pursuit. Garin threw himself flat on the balcony and dropped the jeweled strap of his belt over the lip.

A moment later it snapped taut and he stiffened to an upward pull. Already Dandtan's heels were above the snapping jaws of a morgel. The flier caught the youth around the shoulders and heaved. They rolled together against the wall.

"They are gone! All of them!" Dandtan cried, as he regained his feet. He was right; the morgels howled below, but Kepta and his men had vanished.

"Thrala!" Garin exclaimed.

Dandtan nodded. "They have taken her back to the cells. They believe her safe there."

"Then they think wrong." Garin stopped to pick up the green rod. His companion laughed.

"We'd best start before they get prepared for us."

Garin picked up the Ana. "Which way?"

Dandtan showed him a passage leading from behind the other door. Then he dodged into a side chamber to return with two of the winged cloaks and cloth hoods, so that they might pass as Black Ones.

They went by the mouths of three side tunnels, all deserted. None disputed their going. All the Black Ones had withdrawn from this part of the Caves.

Dandtan sniffed uneasily. "All is not well. I fear a trap."

"While we can pass, let us."

The passage curved to the right and they came into an oval room. Again Dandtan shook his head but ventured no protest. Instead he flung open a door and hurried down a short hall.

It seemed to Garin that there were strange rustlings and squeakings in the dark corners. Then Dandtan stopped so short that the American ran into him.

"Here is the guard room—and it is empty!"

Garin looked over his shoulder into a large room. Racks of strange weapons hung on the walls and the sleeping pallets of the guards were stacked evenly, but the men were nowhere to be seen.

They crossed the room and passed beneath an archway.

"Even the bars are not down," observed Dandtan. He pointed overhead. There hung a portcullis of stone. Garin studied it apprehensively. But Dandtan drew him on into a narrow corridor lined on both sides with barred doors.

"The cells," he explained, and withdrew a bar across one door. The portal swung back and they pushed within.

Thrala arose to face them. Forgetting the disguise he wore, Garin drew back, chilled by her icy demeanor. But Dandtan sprang forward and caught her in his arms. She struggled madly until she saw the face beneath her captor's hood, and then she gave a cry of delight and her arms were about his neck.

"Dandtan!"

He smiled. "Even so, but it is the outlander's doing."

She came to Garin, studying his face. "Outlander? So cold a name is not for you, when you have served us so.'' She offered him her hands and he raised them to his lips.

"And how are you named?''

Dandtan laughed. "Thus the eternal curiosity of women!''

"Garin.''

"Garin,'' she repeated. "How like—'' A faint rose glowed beneath her pearl flesh.

Dandtan's hand fell lightly upon his rescuer's shoulder. "Indeed he is like him. From this day let him bear that other's name. Garan, Son of Light.''

"Why not?'' she returned calmly. "After all—''

"The reward which might have been Garan's may be his? Tell him the story of his namesake when we are again in the Caverns—''

Dandtan was interrupted by a frightened squeak from the Ana. Then came a mocking voice.

"So the prey has entered the trap of its own will. How many hunters may boast the same?''

Kepta leaned against the door, the light of vicious mischief dancing in his eyes. Garin dropped his cloak to the floor, but Dandtan must have read what was in his mind, for he caught him by the arm.

"So you have learned that much wisdom while you have dwelt among us, Dandtan? Would that Thrala had done the same. But fair women find me weak.'' He eyed her proud body in a way that would have sent Garin at his throat had Dandtan not held him. "So shall Thrala have a second chance. How would you like to see these men in the Room of Instruments, Lady?''

"I do not fear you,'' she returned. "Thran once made a prophecy, and he never spoke idly. We shall win free—''

"That will be as fate would have it. Meanwhile, I leave you to each other'' He whipped around the

door and slammed it behind him. They heard the
grating of the bar he slid in place. Then his footsteps
died away.

"There goes evil," murmured Thrala softly. "Perhaps it would have been better if Garin had killed
him as he thought to do. We must get away. . . ."

Garin drew the rod from his belt. The green light
motes gathered and clung about its polished length.

"Do not touch the door," Thrala advised, "only
its hinges."

Beneath the tip of the rod the stone became spongy
and flaked away. Dandtan and Garin caught the door
and eased it to the floor. With one quick movement
Thrala caught up Garin's cloak and swirled it about
her, hiding the glitter of her gem-encrusted robe.

There was a curious cold lifelessness about the air
of the corridor, the light-bearing motes vanishing as
if blown out.

"Hurry!" the Daughter urged. "Kepta is with-
drawing the living light, so that we will have to
wander in the dark."

When they reached the end of the hall the light
was quite gone, and Garin bruised his hands against
the stone portcullis which had been lowered. From
somewhere on the other side of the barrier came
rippling laughter.

"Oh, outlander," called Kepta mockingly, "you
will get through easily enough when you remember
your weapon. But the dark you cannot conquer so
easily, nor that which run the halls."

Garin was already busy with the rod. Within five
minutes their way was clear again. But Thrala stopped
them when they would have gone through. "Kepta
has loosed the hunters."

"The hunters?"

"The morgels and—others," explained Dandtan.

"The Black Ones have withdrawn and only death comes this way. And the morgels see in the dark. . . ."

"So does the Ana."

"Well thought of," agreed the son of the Ancient Ones. "It will lead us out."

As if in answer, there came a tug at Garin's belt. Reaching back, he caught Thrala's hand and knew that she had taken Dandtan's. So linked they crossed the guard room. Then the Ana paused for a long time, as if listening. There was nothing to see but the darkness which hung about them like the smothering folds of a curtain.

"Something follows us," whispered Dandtan.

"Nothing to fear," stated Thrala. "It dare not attack. It is, I think, of Kepta's fashioning. And that which has not true life dreads death above all things. It is going—"

There came the sounds of something crawling slowly away.

"Kepta will not try that again," continued the Daughter, disdainfully. "He knew that his monstrosities would not attack. Only in the light are they to be dreaded—and then only because of the horror of their forms."

Again the Ana tugged at its master's belt. They shuffled into the narrow passage beyond. But there remained the sense of things about them in the dark, things which Thrala continued to insist were harmless and yet which filled Garin with loathing.

Then they entered the far corridor into which led the three halls and which ended in the morgel pit. Here, Garin believed, was their greatest danger from the morgels.

The Ana stopped short, dropping back against Garin's thigh. In the blackness appeared two yellow disks, sparks of saffron in their depths. Garin thrust the rod into Thrala's hands.

"What are you doing?" she demanded.

"I'm going to clear the way. It's too dark to use the rod against moving creatures. . . ." He flung the words over his shoulder as he moved toward the unwinking eyes.

4

Escape from the Caves

Keeping his eyes upon those soulless yellow disks, Garin snatched off his hood, wadding it into a ball. Then he sprang. His fingers slipped on smooth hide, sharp fangs ripped his forearm, blunt nails scraped his ribs. A foul breath puffed into his face and warm slaver trickled down his neck and chest. But his plan succeeded.

The cap was wedged into the morgel's throat and the beast was slowly choking. Blood dripped from Garin's torn flesh, but he held on grimly until he saw the light fade from those yellow eyes. The dying morgel made a last mad plunge for freedom, dragging his attacker along the rock floor. Then Garin felt the heaving body rest limply against his own. He staggered against the wall, panting.

"Garin!" cried Thrala. Her questing hand touched his shoulder and crept to his face. "It is well with you?"

"Yes," he panted. "Let's go on."

Thrala's fingers had lingered on his arm and now

she walked beside him, her cloak making whispering sounds as it brushed against the wall and floor.

"Wait," she cautioned suddenly. "The morgel pit . . ."

Dandtan slipped by them, whispering, "I will try the door."

In a moment he was back. "It is open."

"Kepta believes," mused Thrala, "that we will keep to the safety of the gallery. Therefore let us go through the pit. The morgels will be gone to better hunting grounds."

Through the pit they went. A choking stench arose from underfoot and they trod very carefully. They climbed the stairs on the far side unchallenged, Dandtan leading.

"The rod here, Garin," he called; "this door is barred."

Garin pressed the weapon into Dandtan's hand and leaned against the rock. He was sick and dizzy. The long, deep wounds on his arm and shoulder ached with a biting throb.

When they went on he panted with effort. They still moved in darkness and his distress passed unnoticed.

"This is wrong," he muttered, half to himself. "We go too easily—"

And he was answered out of the blackness. "Well noted, outlander. But you go free for the moment, as do Thrala and Dandtan. Our full accounting is not yet. And now, farewell, until we meet again in the Hall of Thrones. I could find it in me to applaud your courage, outlander. Perhaps you will come to serve me yet."

Garin turned and threw himself toward the voice, rushing up with bruising force against the wall. Kepta laughed.

"Not with the skill of the bull Tand will you capture me."

His second laugh was cut cleanly off, as if a door had been closed. In silence the three hurried up the ramp. Then, as through a curtain, they came into the light of Tav.

Thrala let her drab cloak fall, stood with arms outstretched in the crater land. Her sparkling robe sheathed her in glory and she sang softly, rapt in her own delight. Then Dandtan put his arm about her; she clung to him, staring about as might a beauty-bewildered child.

Garin wondered dully how he would be able to make the journey back to the Caverns when his arm and shoulder were being eaten with a consuming fire. The Ana crept closer to him, peering into his white face.

They were aroused by a howl from the Caves. Thrala cried and Dandtan answered her unspoken question. "They have set the morgels on our trail!"

The howl from the Caves was echoed from the forest. Morgels before and behind them! Garin might set himself against one, Dandtan another, and Thrala could defend herself with the rod, but in the end the pack would kill them.

"We shall claim protection from the Gibi of the Cliff. By the law they must give us aid," said Thrala as, turning up her long robe, she began to run toward the cliffs. Garin picked up the cloak and drew it across his shoulder to hide his welts. When he could no longer match her pace Thrala must not guess the reason for his falling behind.

Garin afterward remembered little of that flight through the forest. At last the gurgle of water broke upon his pounding ears, as he stumbled along a good ten lengths behind his companions. They had come

to the edge of the wood along the banks of the
river.

Without hesitation Thrala and Dandtan plunged
into the oily flood, swimming easily for the other
side. Garin dropped the cloak, wondering if once he
stepped into the yellow stream he would be able to
struggle out again. Already the Ana was paddling in
circles near the shore and pleading with him to follow. Wearily Garin waded out.

The water, which washed the blood and sweat
from his aching body, was faintly brackish and stung
his wounds to life. He could not fight the sluggish
current and it bore him downstream, well away from
where the others landed.

But at last he managed to win free, crawling out
near where a smaller stream joined the river. There
he lay panting facedown upon the moss. And there
they found him, water dripping from his bedraggled
finery, the Ana stroking his muddied hair. Thrala
cried out with concern and pillowed his head on her
knees while Dandtan examined his wounds.

"Why did you not tell us?" demanded Thrala.

He did not try to answer, content to lie there, her
arms supporting him. Dandtan disappeared into the
forest, returning soon, his hands filled with a mass of
crushed leaves. With these he plastered Garin's
wounds.

"You'd better go on," Garin warned.

Dandtan shook his head. "The morgels cannot
swim. If they cross they must go to the bridge, and
that is half the crater away."

The Ana dropped into their midst, its small hand
filled with clusters of purple fruit. And so they feasted,
Garin at ease on a fern couch, accepting food from
Thrala's hand.

There seemed to be some virtue in Dandtan's leaf

plaster for, after a short rest, Garin was able to get to
his feet with no more than a twinge or two in his
wounds. But they started on at a more sober pace.
Through mossy glens and sunlit glades where strange
flowers made perfume, the trail led. The stream they
followed branched twice before they struck away from
the guiding water across the meadow land toward the
crater wall.

Suddenly Thrala threw back her head and gave a
shrill, sweet whistle. Out of the air dropped a yellow
and black insect, as large as a hawk. Twice it circled
her head and then perched itself on her outstretched
wrist.

Its swollen body was jet black, its curving legs,
three to a side, chrome yellow. The round head
ended in a sharp beak and it had large, many-faceted
eyes. The wings, which lazily tested the air, were
black and touched with gold.

Thrala rubbed the round head while the insect
nuzzled affectionately at her cheek. Then she held
out her wrist again and it was gone.

"We shall be expected now and may pass unmo-
lested."

Shortly they became aware of a murmuring sound.
The crater wall loomed ahead, dwarfing the trees at
its base.

"There is the city of the Gibi," remarked Dandtan.

Clinging to the rock were the towers and turrets of
many eight-sided cells.

"They were preparing for the Mists," observed
Thrala. "We shall have company on our journey to
the Caverns."

They passed the trees and reached the foot of the
wax skyscrapers which towered dizzily above their
heads. A great cloud of the Gibi hovered about them.
Garin felt the soft brush of their wings against his

body. And they crowded each other jealously to be near Thrala.

The soft hush-hush of their wings filled the clearing as one large Gibi of outstanding beauty approached. The commoners fluttered off and Thrala greeted the Queen of the cells as an equal. Then she turned to her companions with the information the Gibi Queen had to offer.

"We are just in time. Tomorrow the Gibi leave. The morgels have crossed the river and are out of control. Instead of hunting us they have gone to ravage the forest lands. All Tav has been warned against them. But they may be caught by the Mist and so destroyed. We are to rest in the cliff hollows, and a Gibi shall come for us when it is time to leave."

Garin was awakened by a loud murmuring. Dandtan knelt beside him.

"We must go. Even now the Gibi seal the last of the cells."

They ate hurriedly of grain and honey cakes, and, as they feasted, the Queen again visited them. The first of the swarm were already winging eastward.

With the Gibi nation hanging like a storm cloud above them, the three started off across the meadow. The purple-blue haze was thickening and here and there curious formations, like the dust devils of the desert, arose and danced and disappeared again. The tropic heat of Tav increased; it was as if the ground itself were steaming.

"The Mists draw close; we must hurry," panted Dandtan.

They traversed the tongue of forest which bordered the meadow and came to the central plain of Tav.

There was a brooding stillness. The Ana, perched on Garin's shoulder, shivered.

Their walk became a trot; the Gibi bunched together. Once Thrala caught her breath in a half sob.

"They were flying slowly because of us. And it is so far—"

"Look!" Dandtan pointed at the plain. "The morgels!"

The morgel pack, driven by fear, ran in leaping bounds. They passed within a hundred yards of the three, yet did not turn from their course, although several snarled at them.

"They are already dead," observed Dandtan. "There is no time for them to reach the shelter of the Caves."

Splashing through a shallow brook, the three began to run. For the first time Thrala faltered and broke pace. Garin thrust the Ana into Dandtan's arms and, before she could protest, swept the girl into his arms.

The haze was denser now, settling upon them as a curtain. Black hair, finer than silk, whipped across Garin's throat. Thrala's head was on his shoulder, her heaving breasts arched as she gasped the sultry air.

Then abruptly they tumbled into a throng of the Folk, one of whom reached for Thrala with a crooning cry. It was Sera welcoming her mistress.

Thrala was borne away by the women, leaving Garin with a feeling of desolation.

"The Mists, outlander." It was Urg, pointing toward the Cavern mouth. Two of the Folk swung their weight on a lever. Across the opening a sheet of crystal clicked into place. The Caverns were sealed.

The haze was now inky black outside and billows of it beat against the protecting barrier. It might have been midnight of the blackest, most starless night.

"So will it be for forty days. What is without—dies," said Urg.

"Then we have forty days in which to prepare." Garin spoke his thought aloud. Dandtan's keen face lightened.

"Well said, Garin. Forty days before Kepta may seek us. And we have much to do. But first, our respects to the Lord of the Folk."

Together they went to the Hall of Thrones where, when he saw Dandtan, Trar arose and held out his jade-tipped rod of office. The son of the Ancient Ones touched it.

"Hail! Dweller in the Light, and outlander who has fulfilled the promise of Thran. Thrala is once more within the Caverns. Now you must send this black throne to dust. . . ."

Garin drew the destroying rod from his belt, but Dandtan shook his head. "The time is not yet, Trar. Kepta must finish the pattern he began. We have forty days and then the Black Ones will come."

Trar considered thoughtfully. "So that is to be the way of it. Tharn did not see another war. . . ."

"But he saw an end to Kepta!"

Trar straightened as if some burden had rolled from his thin shoulders. "You speak well, Lord. When there is one to sit upon the Rose Throne, what have we to fear? Listen, oh ye Folk, the Light has returned to the Caverns!"

His cry was echoed by the gathering of the Folk.

"And now, Lord"—he turned to Dandtan with deference—"what are your commands?"

"For the space of one sleep I shall enter the Chamber of Renewing with this outlander, who is no longer an outlander, but one Garin, accepted by the Daughter according to the law. And while we rest let all be made ready. . . ."

"The Dweller in the Light has spoken!" Trar himself escorted them from the Hall.

They came, through many winding passages, to a deep pool of water, in the depths of which lurked odd purple shadows. Dandtan stripped and plunged in, Garin following his example. The water was tinglingly alive and they did not linger in it long. From it they went to a bubble room such as the one Garin had rested in after the bath of light rays; on the cushions in its center they stretched their tired bodies.

When Garin awoke he experienced the same exultation he had felt before. Dandtan regarded him with a smile. "Now to work," he said, as he reached out to press a knob set in the wall.

Two of the Folk appeared, bringing with them clean trappings. After they dressed and ate, Dandtan started for the laboratories. Garin would have gone with him, but Sera intercepted them.

"The Daughter would like to speak with Lord Garin. . . ."

Dandtan laughed. "Go," he ordered. "Thrala's commands may not be slighted."

The Hall of Women was deserted. And the corridor beyond, roofed and walled with slabs of rose-shot crystal, was as empty. Sera drew aside a golden curtain and they were in the Daughter's audience chamber.

A semi-circular dais of the clearest crystal, heaped with rose and gold cushions, faced them. Before it, a fountain, in the form of a flower nodding on a curved stem, sent a spray of water into a shallow basin. The walls of the room were divided into alcoves by marble pillars, each one curved in the semblance of a tree frond.

From the domed ceiling, on chains of twisted gold, seven lamps, each wrought from a single yellow sapphire, gave soft light. The floor was a mosaic of gold and crystal.

Two small Anas, who had been playing among the cushions, pattered up to exchange greetings with Garin's. But of the mistress of the chamber there was no sign. Garin turned to Sera, but before he could phrase his question, she asked mockingly:

"Who is the Lord Garin that he cannot wait with patience?" But she left in search of the Daughter.

Garin glanced uneasily about the room. The jeweled chamber was no place for him. He had started toward the door when Thrala stepped within.

"Greetings to the Daughter." His voice sounded formal and cold, even to himself.

Her hands, which had been held out in welcome, dropped to her sides. A ghost of a frown marred her beauty.

"Greetings, Garin," she returned slowly.

"You sent for me—" he prompted, eager to escape from this jewel box and the unattainable treasure it held.

"Yes." The coldness of her tone was of an exile. "I wished to know how you fared and whether your wounds yet troubled you."

He looked down at his own smooth flesh, cleanly healed by the wisdom of the Folk. "I am myself again and eager to be at such work as Dandtan can find for me. . . ."

Her robe seemed to hiss across the floor as she turned upon him. "Then you had better go—now," she ordered.

And blindly he obeyed. She had spoken as if to a servant, one whom she could summon and dismiss by whim. Even if Dandtan held her love, she might have extended him her friendship. But he knew within him that friendship would be a poor crumb beside the feast for which his pulses pounded.

There was a pattering of feet behind him. So, she would call him back! His pride sent him on. But it was Sera. Her head thrust forward until she truly resembled a reptile.

"Fool! Morgel!" she spat. "Even the Black Ones did not treat her so. Get you out of the Place of Women lest they divide your skin among them!"

Garin ignored her torrent of reproach as well as he could. He seized upon one of the Folk as guide and sought the laboratories. Far beneath the surface of Tav, where the light-motes shone ghostly in the gloom, they came into a place of ceaseless activity, where there were tables crowded with instruments, coils of glass and metal tubing, and other equipment and supplies. This was the focusing point for ceaseless streams of the Folk. On a platform at the far end, Garin saw the tall son of the Ancient Ones working on a framework of metal and shining crystal.

Dandtan glanced up in greeting as Garin joined him. Soon he was issuing instructions—and thus Garin became extra hands and feet for Dandtan. They worked feverishly to build their defenses against the lifting of the Mists. Since there was no day or night in the laboratories, they were able to work steadily for long periods. Twice they went to the Chamber of Renewing, but save for these trips to the upper ways they were not out of the laboratories through all those days. Of Thrala there was no sign, nor did anyone speak of her.

The Cavern dwellers were depending upon two defenses: an evil green liquid, to be thrown in frail glass globes, and a screen charged with energy. Shortly before the lifting of the Mists, these arms were transported to the entrance and installed there. Dandtan and Garin made a last inspection.

"Kepta makes the mistake of underrating his enemies," Dandtan reflected, feeling the edge of the screen caressingly. "When I was captured, on the day my people died, I was sent to the Black Ones' laboratories so that their knowledge seekers might learn the secrets of the Ancient Ones. But I proved a better pupil than teacher and I discovered the defense against the Black Fire. After I had learned that, Kepta grew impatient with my supposed stupidity and tried to use me to force Thrala to his will. For that, as for other things, shall he pay—and the payment will not be in coin of his own striking. Let us think of that. . . ." He turned to greet Urg and Trar and the other leaders of the Folk, who had approached unnoticed.

Among them stood Thrala, her gaze fixed upon the crystal wall between them and the thinning Mist. She noticed Garin no more than she did the Anas playing with her train and the women whispering behind her. But Garin stepped back into the shadows—and what he saw was not weapons of war, but cloudy black hair and graceful white limbs veiled in splendor.

Urg and one of the other chieftains bore down upon the door lever. With a protesting squeak, the glass wall disappeared into the rock. The green of Tav beckoned them out to walk in its freshness; it was renewed with lusty life. But in all that expanse of meadow and forest there was a strange stillness.

"Post sentries," ordered Dandtan. "The Black Ones will come soon."

He beckoned Garin forward as he spoke to Thrala: "Let us go to the Hall of Thrones."

But the Daughter did not answer his smile. "It is not fitting that we should spend time in idle talk. Let

us go instead to call upon the help of those who have
gone before us.'' So speaking, she darted a glance at
Garin as chill as the arctic lands beyond the lip of
Tav, and then swept away with Sera bearing her
train.

Dandtan stared at Garin. "What has happened between you two?"

Garin shook his head. "I don't know. No man is
born with an understanding of women—"

"But she is angered with you. You must know
why."

For a moment Garin was tempted to tell the truth:
that he dared not break any barrier she chose to raise,
lest he seize what in honor was none of his. But he
shook his head mutely. Neither of them saw Thrala
again until Death entered the Caverns.

5

The Battle in the Caverns

Garin stood with Dandtan looking out into the plain of
Tav. Some distance away were two slender steel-
tipped towers which were, in reality, but hollow
tubes filled with the Black Fire. Before these, dark-
clad figures were busy.

"They seem to believe us already defeated. Let
them think so," commented Dandtan, touching the
screen they had erected before the Cavern entrance.

As he spoke, Kepta swaggered through the tall
grass to call a greeting: "Ho, rock dweller, I would
like to speak with you—"

Dandtan edged around the screen, Garin a pace
behind.

"I see you, Kepta."

"Good. I trust that your ears will serve you as well
as your eyes. These are my terms: Give Thrala to me to
dwell in my chamber and the outlander to provide sport
for my captains. Make no resistance but throw open the
Caverns so that I may take my rightful place in the Hall
of Thrones. Do this and we shall be at peace. . . ."

Dandtan stood unmovingly before the screen. "And this is our reply: Return to the Caves; break down the bridge between your land and ours. Let no Black One come hither again, ever. . . ."

Kepta laughed. "So, that is your decision! Then this is what we shall do: Take Thrala, to be mine for a space and then go to my captains—"

Garin hurled himself forward, felt Kepta's lips mash beneath his fist; his fingers were closing about the other's throat as Dandtan, who was trying to pull him away from his prey, shouted a warning: "Watch out!"

A morgel had leaped from the grass, its teeth snapping about Garin's wrist, forcing him to drop Kepta. Then Dandtan laid it senseless by a sharp blow with his belt.

On hands and knees Kepta crawled back to his men. The lower part of his face was a red and dripping smear. He screamed an order with savage fury.

Dandtan drew the still raging Garin behind the screen. "Be a little prudent," he panted. "Kepta can be dealt with in other ways than with bare hands."

The towers were swinging their tips toward the entrance. Dandtan ordered the screen wedged tightly into place.

Outside, the morgel Dandtan had stunned got groggily to its feet. When it had limped half the distance back to its master, Kepta gave the order to fire. The broad beam of black light from the tip of the nearest tower caught the beast head on. There was a chilling scream of agony, and where the morgel had been gray ashes drifted on the wind.

A loud crackling arose as the black beam struck the screen and was reflected off. Green grass beneath seared away, leaving only parched earth and naked

blue soil. Those within the Cavern crouched behind
their frail protection, half blinded by the light from
the seared grass, coughing from the chemical-ridden
fumes which curled about the cracks of the rock.

Then the beam faded out. Thin smoke plumed
from the tips of the towers and steam arose from the
blackened ground. Dandtan drew a deep breath.

"It held!" he cried, betraying at last the fear
which had ridden him.

Men of the Folk dragged engines of tubing before
the screen, while others brought forth the globes of
green liquid. Dandtan stood aside, as if this matter
were the business of the Folk alone, and Garin recalled that the Ancient Ones were opposed to the
taking of life.

Trar was in command now. At his orders the
globes were placed on spoon-shaped holders. Loopholes in the screen clicked open. Trar brought down
his hand in signal. The globes arose lazily, sliding
through the loopholes and floating out toward the
towers.

One, aimed short, struck the ground where the fire
had burned it bare, and broke. The liquid came forth,
sluggishly, forming a gray-green gas as the air struck
it. Another spiral of gas arose almost at the foot of
one of the towers—and then another. . . .

Quickly, a tortured screaming followed which soon
faded to a weak yammering. They could see shapes,
no longer human or animal, staggering about in the
fog.

Dandtan turned away, his face white with horror.
Garin's hands were over his ears to shut out that
crying.

At last it was quiet; there was no more movement
by the towers. Urg placed a sphere of rosy light upon
the nearest machine and flipped it out into the enemy

camp. As if it were a magnet it drew the green tendrils of gas to itself and left the air clear. Here and there lay shrunken, livid shapes, the towers brooding over them.

One of the Folk burst into their midst, a woman of Thrala's following.

"Haste!" She clawed at Garin. "Kepta takes Thrala!"

She ran wildly back the way she had come, with the American pounding at her heels. They burst into the Hall of Thrones and saw a struggling group before the dais.

Garin heard someone howl like an animal, became aware the sound came from his own throat. For the second time his fist found its mark on Kepta's face. With a shriek of rage the Black One released Thrala and sprang at Garin, his nails tearing gashes in the flier's face. Twice Garin twisted free and sent bone-crushing blows into the other's ribs. Then he got the grip he wanted and his fingers closed around Kepta's throat. In spite of the Black One's struggles he held on until a limp body rolled beneath him.

Panting, Garin pulled himself up from the blood-stained floor and grabbed the arm of the Jade Throne for support.

"Garin!" Thrala's arms were about him, her pitying fingers on his wounds. And in that moment he forgot Dandtan, forgot everything he had steeled himself to remember. She was in his arms and his mouth sought hers possessively. Nor was she unresponsive, but yielded as a flower yields to the wind.

"Garin!" she whispered softly. Then, almost shyly, she broke away.

Beyond her stood Dandtan, his face white, his mouth tight. Garin remembered. And a little mad with pain and longing, he dropped his eyes, trying not to see the loveliness that was Thrala.

"So, outlander, Thrala flies to your arms—"

Garin turned quickly. Kepta was hunched on the broad seat of the jet throne.

"No, I am not dead, outlander—nor shall you kill me, as you think to do. I go now, but I shall return. We have met and hated, fought and died before—you and I. You were a certain Garan, Marshal of the Air Fleet of Yu-Lac on a vanished world, and I was Lord of Koom. That was in the days before the Ancient Ones pioneered space. You and I and Thrala, we are bound together and even fate cannot break those bonds. Farewell, Garin. And you, Thrala, remember the ending of that other Garan. It was not an easy one."

With a last malicious chuckle, he leaned back in the throne. His battered body slumped. Then the hard lines of the throne blurred; it shimmered in the light. Abruptly then both it and its occupant were gone. They were staring at empty space, above which loomed the rose throne of the Ancient Ones.

"He spoke true," murmured Thrala. "We have had other lives, other meetings—so will we meet again. But for the present he returns to the darkness that sent him forth. It is finished."

Without warning, a low rumbling filled the Cavern; the walls rocked and swayed. Lizard and human, they huddled together until the swaying stopped. Finally a runner appeared with news that one of the Gibi had discovered that the Caves of Darkness had been sealed by an underground quake. The menace of the Black Ones was definitely at an end.

Although there were falls of rock within the Caverns and some of the passages were closed, few of the Folk suffered injury. Gibi scouts reported that the land about the entrance to the Caves had sunk, and that the River of Gold, thrown out of its bed, was fast filling this basin to form a lake.

As far as they could discover, none of the Black Ones had survived the battle and the sealing of the Caves. But they could not be sure that there was not a handful of outlaws somewhere within the confines of Tav.

The crater itself was changed. A series of raw hills had appeared in the central plain. The pool of boiling mud had vanished and trees in the forest lay flat, as if cut by a giant scythe.

Upon their return to the cliff city, the Gibi found most of their wax skyscrapers in ruins, but they set about rebuilding without complaint. The squirrel-farmers emerged from their burrows and were again busy in the fields.

Garin felt out of place in all the activity that filled the Caverns. More than ever he was the outlander with no true roots in Tav. Restlessly, he explored the Caverns, spending many hours in the Place of Ancestors, where he studied those men of the outer world who had preceded him into this weird land.

One night when he came back to his chamber he found Dandtan and Trar awaiting him there. There was a curious hardness in Dandtan's attitude, a somber sobriety in Trar's carriage.

"Have you sought the Hall of Women since the battle?" demanded the son of the Ancient Ones abruptly.

"No," retorted Garin shortly, wondering if Dandtan was accusing him of double dealing.

"Have you sent a message to Thrala?"

Garin held back his rising temper. "I have not ventured where I cannot."

Dandtan nodded to Trar as if his suspicions had been confirmed. "You see how it stands, Trar."

Trar shook his head slowly. "But never has the summoning been at fault—"

"You forget," Dandtan reminded him sharply. "It was once—and the penalty was exacted. So shall it be again."

Garin looked from one to the other, confused. Dandtan seemed possessed of a certain ruthless anger, but Trar was manifestly unhappy.

"It must come after council, the Daughter willing," the Lord of the Folk said.

Dandtan strode toward the door. "Thrala is not to know. Assemble the council tonight. Meanwhile, see that he"—he jerked his thumb toward Garin—"does not leave this room."

Thus Garin became a prisoner under the guard of the Folk, unable to discover of what Dandtan accused him, or how he had aroused the hatred of the Cavern ruler. Unless Dandtan's jealousy had been aroused and he was determined to rid himself of a rival.

Believing this, the American went willingly to the chamber where the judges waited. Dandtan sat at the head of a long table, Trar at his right and lesser nobles of the Folk beyond.

"You know the charge." Dandtan's words were tipped with venom as Garin came to stand before him. "Out of his own mouth has this outlander condemned himself. Therefore I ask that you decree for him the fate of that outlander of the second calling who rebelled against the summoning."

"The outlander has admitted his fault?" questioned one of the Folk.

Trar inclined his head sadly. "He did."

As Garin opened his mouth to demand a statement of the charge against him, Dandtan spoke again:

"What say you, Lords?"

For a long moment they sat in silence and then they bobbed their lizard heads in assent. "Do as you desire, Dweller in the Light."

Dandtan smiled without mirth. "Look, outlander." He passed his hand over the glass of the seeing mirror set in the table top. "This is the fate of a rebel—"

In the shining surface Garin saw pictured a break in Tav's wall. At its foot stood a group of men of the Ancient Ones, and in their midst struggled a prisoner. They were forcing him to climb the crater wall. Garin watched him reach the lip and crawl over, to stagger across the steaming rock, dodging the scalding vapor of hot springs, until he pitched down in the slimy mud.

"Such was his ending, and so will you end—"

The calm brutality of that statement aroused Garin's anger. "Rather would I die that way than linger in this den," he cried hotly. "You, who owe your life to me, would send me to such a death without even telling me of what I am accused. Little is there to choose between you and Kepta, after all—except that he was an open enemy!"

Dandtan sprang to his feet, but Trar caught his arm.

"He speaks fairly. Ask him why he will not fulfill the summoning."

While Dandtan hesitated, Garin leaned across the table, flinging his words, weapon-like, straight into that cold face.

"I'll admit that I love Thrala—have loved her since that moment when I saw her on the steps of the morgel pit in the Caves. Since when has it become a crime to love that which may not be yours—if you do not try to take it?"

Trar released Dandtan, his golden eyes gleaming. "If you love her, claim her. It is your right."

"Do I not know"—Garin turned to him—"that she is Dandtan's? Thran had no idea of Dandtan's survival when he laid his will upon her. Shall I stoop to holding her to an unwelcome bargain? Let her go to the one she loves. . . ."

Dandtan's face was livid, and his hands, resting on the table, trembled. One by one the Lords of the Folk slipped away, leaving the two face to face.

"And I thought to order you to your death." Dandtan's whisper was husky as it emerged between dry lips. "Garin, we thought you knew—and, knowing, had refused her."

"Knew what?"

"That I am Thran's son—and Thrala's brother."

The floor swung beneath Garin's unsteady feet. Dandtan's hands were warm on his shoulders.

"I am a fool," said the American slowly.

Dandtan smiled. "A very honorable fool! Now you get to Thrala, who deserves to hear the full of this tangle."

So it was, with Dandtan by his side, that Garin walked for the second time down that hallway, to pass the golden curtains and stand in the presence of the Daughter. She came straight from her cushions into his arms when she read what was in his face. They needed no words.

And in that hour began Garin's life in Tav.

PART TWO

1

Lord of Yu-Lac

Often have I (who was Garin Featherstone in the world beyond the Mist Barrier, and am now Garan of the Flame, mate to that Royal Lady, Thrala, Daughter of the Ancient Ones) listened to the half-forgotten tales of that regal race who fled from a dying planet across the void of space to land upon the antarctic continent of our young world and blast out there the great crater of Tav for their future dwelling place.

From time to time, we are told, they renewed the vigor of their line by calling certain men from the world outside the barriers they had erected. I had been one of those so called. But I came in a later age and in a dark time. For evil had come into the crater and conflict riven apart the dwellers therein. And now at present, since that crushing defeat we wreaked with the help of outraged nature upon Kepta, Lord of the Black Flame, and those who followed him, but two of the Ancient Race remain, my lady wife and her brother Dandtan.

At the moment of his overthrow Kepta had made

certain dark promises concerning our uncertain future
and also some gibing reference to the far past which
had caught my interest. For he said that the three of
us, Thrala, Kepta, and I, were bound together. We
had lived and fought before, even as we would live
and fight again.

There is a Garan who lies in the Cavern of the
Sleepers and whose story Thrala has told me. But
before him—long before—there were others.

For when I questioned the Daughter about Kepta's
words, she took me into one of the curious bubble-
like rooms where are mirrors of seeing embedded in
tables. And there she seated herself on a cushioned
bench, drawing me down beside her.

"Far and long have we come, beloved," she said
softly, "but not so far or not so long that I cannot
recall the beginning. And you remember?"

"Nothing," I answered, my eyes on the mirror.

She sighed. "Perhaps this is but just—mine was
the fault—so mine the burden of memory. What we
did, we two, in the great city of Yu-Lac on the
vanished world of Krand, has lain between us for
long—long. It being gone at last, I half fear to
summon it again."

I arose abruptly.

"Let it be then."

"Nay!" She caught my hand. "We have paid the
price, three times over have we paid it. Once in Yu-Lac
and twice in the Caverns. Our unhappiness is gone,
and now it pleases me to look again upon the most
splendid act I have ever witnessed. Behold, my Lord."

She raised her slender hands above the mirror. It
misted.

I stood on a fancifully carved balcony of opalescent stone looking down upon a fantastic city not yet

awakened from the hours of sleep. In the rosy sky, strange to my half-earthly eyes and yet familiar, were the first golden strands of earthly dawn. Yu-Lac, the Mighty, lay below me and I was Lord Garan, Marshal of the Emperor's Air Fleet, peer of the Empire.

By birth I had no right to either title or position, for my mother had been a lady of the court and my father an officer. They broke the law forbidding mating between different clans and castes by their secret marriage and so doomed me from birth to be one of the wards of the state and the lowliest of the low.

Luckily for me, and those unfortunates like me, the Emperor Fors, when he ascended the Rose Throne in the Palace of Light, issued a decree opening army service to state wards. In my fifteenth year I made my choice and submitted myself to the military brand.

The life was a hard one, but it was escape from far worse and—having some ambition and ability, doubtless inherited from my father—I rose step by step. Fourteen years later I was Marshal of the Imperial Air Fleet and a military lord, created so by the Emperor's own hand.

But the soldier who stood on the balcony, looking down upon the wondrous beauty which was Yu-Lac in the dawn, was neither happy nor contented. All his hard-won honors were no more to him than the diverse scars which seamed his flesh. For he had dared (though no man knew it) to raise his eyes and heart to one as far above him as Krand's red sun was above her yellow fields.

I, a veteran of countless small border wars and raiding parties, was as lovesick and despondent as the youngest and most callow recruit uneasily slumbering in the barracks below my tower. Though I resolutely put aside my unholy longing throughout the day, yet at night and in the dawning my memory

and dreams broke loose from control, nor did I try
too hard to leash them.

Like the pentitent priests in the great temple of On
I tortured myself by memories which inflicted twice
the pain of any body hurt. By my companions I was
counted a seasoned warrior, cold of heart and unin-
terested in aught but the pressing affairs of my office.
And yet—

Three years— By On, could it be so long? Then I
had been commander of the Emperor's flagship, the
thrice happy vessel which was selected to bear the
Lady Thrala from her temple school in Toran to her
father's crystal palace which crowned the central hill
of Yu-Lac.

The Imperial Princess had been surrounded by the
countless courtiers of her suite, but one blessed night
she had slipped away from them all and entered the
control cabin where it had been my heaven-directed
whim to stand watch alone. Thrala, not Imperial
Highness, had she been when our snatched hour was
over.

Twice had I seen her since. Once on the day when
I had knelt at the Emperor's feet to receive the staff
of my office and had dared to raise my eyes to that
golden throne at his right hand. And the second? It
was in the royal pleasure gardens where I was awaiting an audience. She had passed with her ladies.
Who was I with the military brand seared deep in my
shoulder muscle to look upon the Peerless One?

The castes of Krand were rigidly ordered. A man
might rise to honor in any one but he could not pass
into another. A peasant might become a lord of the
land and a noble but neither he nor his sons might
serve at court nor in the fleet.

So a soldier of the forces, even though he bore a
title, had no right to long for a daughter of the

Learned Ones. They were our rulers and great nobles, far above the commoners in the breadth of their knowledge. They had as much ability to harness and bend to their will both men and natural forces as I had over the mindless slaves of the fields, that subhuman race which the Learned Ones had produced in the laboratories. They were a race apart, blessed—or cursed—with superhuman powers.

But Thrala was my beloved and all the decrees of the Emperor and the chains of ancient custom could not alter that fact nor blot her image from my heart. I think I would have finished out my life, content at last only to worship my dreams of her, had not brooding Fate decided a far different future for all the pigmy men creatures who crawled about that globe which was Krand.

That morning I was not left long to indulge in self-pity and fruitless longings. A tiny bell chimed in the room behind me, giving notice that someone desired to enter my sleeping chamber. I crossed to the disk on the wall and ran my hand across it. Upon its polished surface then appeared the likeness of my aide-de-camp, that young rascal, Anatan of Hol.

"Enter," I said into the mouth tube beside the disk, my voice thus unlocking the door.

"Well, scamp, what scrap have you gotten into?" I asked resignedly, being well used to meeting in the early morning a contrite but guilty young officer who wished me to get him out of some entanglement into which his reckless, youthful spirits had plunged him.

"For wonder," he answered brightly, "none. Praise be to On. But there is a messenger from the palace below."

In spite of my self-schooling, my pulse quickened. I turned again to my calling disk and ordered the military clerk in my inner office to assure the messenger that I would receive him as soon as I was properly accoutered.

Anatan busied himself with laying out my trappings and equipment while I splashed in my adjoining bath. He kept up the while a steady chatter of gossip and rumor from both barracks and court.

"Lord Kepta is going to pay us a visit," he said.

I dropped the tunic for which I had reached.

"Kepta of Koom?" I asked shortly, hoping that my perturbation had not been noted.

"Who else? There is only one Kepta of whom I have knowledge." His sudden round-eyed innocence did not deceive me.

But Anatan, for all his careless talk and ways, had ever been loyal to me and I did not fear that he would betray me now. There was no one I hated more than Kepta of Koom, who had the power to crush me like an insect and who would be only too quick to use that same power should he ever suspect the true state of my feelings toward him.

In every pile of fruit there is one piece softer and more inclined to rot than the others—and that same piece unless removed will, in time, corrupt the rest. To my mind the Master of Koom was the rotten piece among the Learned Ones.

He did not mingle much with the rest of his caste fellows but kept close to the huge black stone citadel of his dark, wind-swept city, there carrying on secret experiments in his laboratories far under the crust of Krand. Just what those experiments were, not one of the Learned Ones could tell, but I had my suspicions and they were not pleasant ones. To all knowledge there is both a dark and a light side and, if rumor spoke true, Kepta turned to the dark far oftener than he did to the light. I had heard stories and even traced a tale or two, but without proof what could I do? Lord Kepta was a Learned One by birth and I was a state ward, who by the Emperor's favor had won some fame and position. Should I care to retain both, or even my life, it would be well for me to forget vague stories.

Kepta was highly popular with a certain class of officer in my corps. He entertained lavishly at intervals and his purse was always open to those in temporary financial difficulties. But to my suspicious mind it appeared that he wished to get as many of the soldiers as possible under obligation to him. I had always some civil plea of duty ready in answer to his frequent invitations and, under my guidance, Anatan, and the better sort of his comrades, did likewise.

It was not often, however, that the Master of Koom ventured out of his tall keep. He preferred to entice his company to him, rather than to issue forth to seek it beyond his fortress. But for the past month there had been a mustering of the Learned Ones within Yu-Lac and he had doubtless been summoned to join them by the Emperor.

If he were coming to take his place among his peers he had not been expected so soon, that much I knew. As Commander of the Airport of Yu-Lac, I had been given no warning of his coming so that I might make ready a berth for his private ship among the pleasure and traveling craft of the Emperor's household. His sudden, almost unannounced arrival meant trouble for everyone, I thought impatiently.

I buckled on my jeweled scale armor, made more for ceremonial show than defense, and snapped the catch of my sword belt. From Anatan's hand I took my silver war cloak and left the apartment.

The ramp which led from my private suite to the public offices curled about the center core of the cone-shaped tower in a graceful, though steep, spiral.

Its walls were floridly frescoed with conventionalized scenes of warfare and the chase, occupations always bracketed together in the minds of my race. But here and there mirrors of vision were set deep into the smooth finish of the painted surface so that the passerby might be in instant touch with any part of the great military depot of which the cone tower was the heart.

It pleased me now to check upon the efficiency of my under officers as I passed. Here I caught a glimpse of one of the almost obsolete mounted troops returning from early morning maneuvers. The men rode at ease, their small, scaly-skinned grippon mounts eager for the shelter of the stables, dragging their heavy armored tails in the dust of the parade ground. But two such troops remained and their duties were light— acting as the Emperor's guard when he wished to travel in state.

Commerce, in the persons of the frontier-breaking city merchants, had first demonstrated the advantages of deserting our island-infested seas and mountainous lands for the quicker and easier mode of travel by air. The military was not long in following the example set it. Infantry and grippon troops were speedily disbanded; the arrogant and all-powerful Air Force developed and consolidated its position within a single decade. The navy vanished from the decaying harbors of Krand, unless a handful of ships, rotting as they rolled at anchor, could be dignified by a title which had once been proudly borne by half a million war vessels.

Not content with the profits and the supremacy it had raped from the forces of defense, the Air Ministry was attempting, as I had first suspected and could now prove, to establish an ironbound monopoly. What wild goal they had set for themselves only On knew, and yet, despite all warnings, rulers of Krand refused to stir against them.

I fingered my sword hilt as I went. Men no longer turned to metal to solve their hates and passions; the weapon I wore was but a pretty toy, borne purely as insignia of rank. War meant more subtle armaments— liquids that burned or froze, death which curdled the very air about its victim. And horrors undreamed of by mankind-at-large had been evolved in the distant laboratories. A spark leaping out—what man could foresee the end? And this gathering of the Learned Ones at Yu-Lac. No wild border tribe was in revolt; the five great nations were at peace as they had been for years. It was said on every hand that there was naught to fear— Yet I was troubled and my hand sought my sword hilt by way of reassurance.

The messenger from the palace, a smart young officer attached to the Emperor's guard, was alertly awaiting my arrival.

"The throne desires the presence of the worthy Lord Garan," he recited formally. "He will be pleased to present himself in the Hall of the Nine Princes upon the third hour."

"To hear is to obey, in this as in all things." I murmured the standard reply demanded of a recipient of a royal message.

He slipped to one knee and touched the pavement before me in salute.

At the third hour? Then I still had time to break my fast before I must go. Taking Anatan by the arm I went into the eating chamber used by all those who lodged within the confines of the tower. We took our seat at a polished table which stood with one side tight against the wall. Anatan thrust down a tiny plunger in the table top twice. The wall panel facing us sank back and our food bowls slid out. The stuff was well flavored and highly nutritious but so prepared with artificial colorings and tastes that no one could ever swear as to the original content of any dish. This fashion, introduced by the overcivilized city dwellers, had never found favor with me and I longed for the cruder but, to me, more succulent dishes one found set out in the frontier camps or in small country inns.

The city dwellers, sated as they were in all the refinements life could offer, had lost many of the true joys of living. Their scented "pleasure palaces" were regarded with a sort of righteous horror by the sturdy country folk. And, unless the many tales we heard were ill-founded, the secret police might indeed have found much to interest them in one of those beautiful, almost dreamlike, castles.

As if he had read the thoughts passing through my mind, Anatan broke the silence.

"There is a new 'palace' in the Sotan quarter."

"So," I observed indulgently. "Did you chance upon it last night?"

He shook his head in mock regret. "It is not for the likes of me. Kanddon of Stal was entering as I passed and I saw Lord Palkun's guards by the door."

"High play then?" I wondered aloud as he named the two most wealthy and influential men below the rank of Learned Ones who maintained residences in Yu-Lac.

"That and other things." He grinned in a knowing manner which ill became his boyish face. "If the Lord Garan visits there would he not be needing a companion?"

"And when, puppy, have I wasted unwise moments behind the curtains of a 'pleasure palace'? But this I promise you"—I spoke lightly enough, not being able to read the future—"when I enter that one in the Sotan you shall be at my side."

"Done! And that is a promise, my Lord," he rapped out eagerly. Thus did we leave it as I clambered into the one-motor flier which was to transport me across the city to a landing stage behind the crystal walls of the Emperor's palace.

2

The Master of Koom

It being yet early morning, the air lanes above the bulk of the city were uncrowded by the pleasure and business craft which would hover, dart down and across, during the later hours. Save for a patrol or two that I passed, no one disputed my course until just before I swung my ship in to land upon the stage by the middle, slanting spire of the citadel.

Then it was that a slim, black two-passenger, whose rakish lines spelled both speed and ease of handling, cut ill-manneredly in before the nose of my ship and came down, with its belly hugging the very landing spot I had marked for my own.

With a hot speech ready for the impudent youngster who had so high-handedly usurped my coveted place, I brought my tiny flier in to berth it beside the shining black speeder. But it was no sprig of the court whom I confronted when I stepped out.

For, with a slight smile holding, to my mind, more than the suspicion of a sneer, curling his finely cut lips, the tall Master of Koom lingered by the entrance to the down ramp. His arrogantly held head was bare of either ceremonial crown or helmet and his crisp black hair was ruffled by the morning wind, the same wind which tugged at the heavy folds of his long orange cloak.

By his side was his air commander, a sulky fellow, Japlan of Toc, who had been held in ill repute among fighting men for many years. He, at least, made no pretense of desiring my friendship, but he scowled so belligerently that the knotted skin of his forehead drew his eyebrows together to form one bushy bar.

"Our worthy Lord Garan," purred Kepta. "May we venture to congratulate the victor of Tarnan upon his exploit? Japlan developed a severe attack of jealousy when the news of your success reached our poor backwater. I marvel yet at his full recovery. It is full, is it not, Japlan?" he baited his surly officer.

"Oh, aye," growled that one, all the while making very plain to read upon his face his true opinion of me and all my works.

My training as a soldier had not fitted me for the tongue- and thought-twisting ways of court speech where one can praise a man fairly to his face when you despise him heartily. So, as my speech was apt to be as blunt at my thoughts, I did not care to play the courtier more than was necessary.

"You do me too much honor, my Lord," I answered, with all the courtesy I could summon. "A word of praise from the Master of Koom is not to be lightly dismissed."

His drooping eyelids lifted a fraction and his smile grew more pronounced.

"Your days at court have polished the soldier to produce the finished courtier, Lord Garan," he observed, and now the sneer was broad and ill-concealed.

A man of my own caste and rank would have felt

my fist grate against his teeth for less. His position held him above my resentment, as well he knew, yet never before had his hostility been so open. I wondered, my blood quickening in my veins, if he had uncovered some trace of my active and inquisitive distrust of him. His mask of good fellowship had cracked and I had seen the real man who was using that mask for his own purposes.

So, though my muscles tensed, I controlled my rising anger. But someday, On willing, I would face that sneering devil man to man.

"I give thanks to the Master of Koom." My reply was as chill as I could make it but still formally polite.

He gathered his cloak closer about his broad shoulders and turned away abruptly with Japlan at his heels. I waited a moment or so, allowing them a start before following them down the ramp.

As I hesitated there, the sleek lines of the Koomian's flier caught my eye and interest. Ships were my life and new designs always held me enthralled. Though I dared not linger to examine it closely, I knew that its shape, especially the outward appearance of its motor compartment, suggested some startling new development, something very different from our most modern product.

Apparently the workmen of the dark northern island had chanced upon some new form of propulsion, producing as a result an engine much smaller and more compact than any I had ever seen.

Reluctantly I tore myself away, knowing that Kepta would suspect if I lingered too long. But I determined, as I set foot upon the ramp, to discover the secret of the trim craft before its master whisked it away from Yu-Lac again.

The ramp ended in a single broad step and then I

was out upon the green and amber pavement which led to the Hall of the Nine Princes. Towering columns of burnished copper supported the roof of the covered passage but the sides were open to the scented winds. To my left, four deep steps of dull green stone cut into the first of the wonder gardens which made the inner hold of the sprawling citadel a place of marvels and delights.

To the right, the steps leading down were steeper, giving access to a bronze landing where a half dozen or so gaily painted skiffs bobbed on the yellow, petal-strewn water of one of the five canals. As it was yet early, none save a solitary guard paced the passage. No lady, in spite of my daring hopes, swayed along the garden paths, or floated petal-wise on the canal. There was only a gentle brooding quiet.

But the Hall of the Nine Princes was occupied when I entered. One of the smaller council chambers and reception rooms of the palace, it was furnished with a massive table, hewn from a single log and treated with the famous carbonizing process of the Emperor's laboratories until it was as hard and durable as the age-old rocks of the Imurian Sea. Precisely in the center of this board, placed so that its occupant faced the single entrance to the chamber, was a chair of the same substance and, on either side of that, backless benches.

By virtue of my position I was well-known to the Emperor and the members of his all-powerful council. For the most part the latter were just, though severe, men, requiring of those under their authority a steadfast and utterly devoted loyalty to the state. Once convinced of my trueness, they had granted me an almost free hand in my own department, asking merely for a semimonthly report. In the past, since I had assumed my high office, our relations had been

friendly enough, though never growing warmer than
the austere formality of the court permitted.

But now there was a change in their attitude. Long
years of almost constant warfare and soldiering had
supplied me with that sixth sense permitted those
who live under the thin hem of Danger's cloak. And
now I felt instantly the tension, the certain chillness,
which met me even as I stepped within.

Whether I stood in personal peril of some sort, or
whether some event beyond my control had aroused
them, I had no means of knowing. But that same
feeling, which had guided my hand to my sword that
morning as I had hurried to meet the Emperor's
messenger, again twitched my fingers toward the
weapon on my hip. I felt the skin across my shoulders roughen. There was trouble here.

"The Marshal of the Fleet greets the Lord of the
Air, the Ruler of the Five Seas, the Beloved of
On—" I began the formal salutation.

"Enough." The Emperor's voice severed my greeting dryly. "Be seated, Lord Garan—there." He motioned toward a stool some six paces to the right of
where I stood. I obeyed, but now my tongue moved
in a mouth suddenly gone dry. There was danger
here—to *me!*

"You maintain a secret system of information, do
you not?"

"Aye, Great One. That being part of my duties."

"And is this also part of your duties?" He handed
two metal plates to the attendant at his side. The man
arose from his seat and, passing around the table,
came to stand before me, holding what he bore so
that I might look upon it.

Incised in the soft surface of the metal were draw-
ings and formulas totally strange to me. Wholly bewil-

dered, I raised my eyes to the cold mask which was the Emperor's face.

"I have never seen these before, Sire. Nor do I understand their meaning."

"And yet they were discovered among the private records of your intelligence office," he answered meaningly.

I faced him squarely. "I repeat, Great One, I have not seen these before."

Whereupon Malkus of Throt, a lean, bare bone of a man, totally devoid of all the softer emotions, cackled faintly behind his skinny hand. That evil parody of a man's full-throated laughter aroused me, doubtless even as he had intended.

"Is the Marshal of the Fleet standing trial for wrongdoing, Great One? I beg you, my Lords, be a little plainer with your servant."

The Emperor frowned. "A complaint has been lodged against this nation and you by the men of Koom—"

Koom! The name burst red-hot in my mind. Koom! Then I had been right in assigning some devilish meaning to Kepta's unannounced arrival.

"Certain private matters of the Master have been spied upon—"

I started. There my conscience was not clear. I had been searching for the key to the dark riddle of Kepta. Of that I was guilty.

"And now, even as Lord Kepta had foretold, these are found among your records." The Emperor's mouth was grim.

"Sir, and my Lords, I can only say as I have before, these plates you show me I have never before seen. If they were found among the records of the Fleet, I have no knowledge of how they came to be there. But I promise you"—I ended through twisted

lips—"that I shall not be long in delving to the
bottom of this strange matter."

Malkus cackled again, his thin screech of indecent
mirth echoing through the chamber. "Behold virtue
aroused," he mouthed in glee.

I rounded upon him swiftly. "You mock me, my
Lord?"

He shrugged but vouched me no other answer. I
rose to my feet. With steady hands I unfastened the
buckle of my sword belt and drew it from around me.

"Since, Great One, it seems that I am no longer
worthy of your trust, I will give back into your hands
this symbol of my office. I was naught but a plain
soldier, and a soldier am I content to be. Little do I
know of government policies, but in my thoughts it is
clear that a scapegoat is desired for some matter of
state. If I can serve Yu-Lac best by my personal
disgrace, I stand ready for orders. For I know that I
have been faithful in all things to the best of my
ability."

"Now that, my Lords, can be said by few in
Yu-Lac today," a voice sped clear across the room. I
turned.

In the doorway stood a man of my own years, a
Learned One by his dress. But even among the Great
Ones I have known but three others with his air of
powerful self-control. The Lady Thrala had it, and
the Emperor, and—Kepta. But the Koomian's was an
alien power unlike the others. Who this newcomer
might be I did not know, but that which is the
innermost part of me, the indestructible part, recognized and hailed a leader of men.

"Greetings, Thran," the Emperor arose.

"And to you, Sire, be peace. Let all be well with
you, my Lords."

With easy grace he crossed the room to stand beside me.

"And now what is this I have chanced upon? Why does the noble captain hand back his sword? With what may any man living reproach Garan of Yu-Lac?"

"But a short while ago," I said bitterly, "I too might have asked an answer to that last question of yours, my Lord."

His eyes met mine and I felt a certain warmth spread through me.

"I have watched you, Lord Garan. And speaking freely before this council I say that there is no other man within the bounds of the inner sea in whom I would sooner place my trust. Thran of Gorl says it!"

The Emperor smiled, a wintery cleft in his mask. "Take up your sword, my Lord. Where proof of wrongdoing is lacking, there can be no arguments for or against a man. But it would be well to get to the heart of this matter, for your own sake. A word spoken into the ear of a wise man is more to be heeded than the whisper of a passing breeze."

Thoroughly bewildered by this sudden about-face, I buckled on my belt and dropped to one knee to touch the floor before the council.

"Have I your leave to depart, Great One?"

The Emperor nodded. I turned to go but somehow I knew Thran's eyes were on my back until I stepped from the chamber. Some game, whose stake or purpose I could not fathom, had been played, or perchance the play had just begun. But that I was a piece in the game I had no doubt.

Still puzzling over that strange meeting in the Hall and the Emperor's parting words, I turned aside into the gardens instead of returning directly to the landing stage and my flier.

Clearly I had been ordered to set my house in

order and produce the person or persons responsible for the appearance of the Koomian documents among my records. I must, without delay, set in motion my secret machinery of observation and deduction.

But my thoughts kept wandering back to the idea that someone had attempted to discredit me with the council, tried to so force me out of my position. That could mean only one thing—I was a menace. The Air Ministers, with their ever-growing power, or Kepta of Koom, from whom every drop of blood within me shrank in revulsion—which moved against me now? For the past year I had been burrowing into the secrets of both, striving to uncover the mysterious something which I *knew* lay there waiting to be discovered.

Somewhere on Krand there was a center of disturbance responsible for every frontier outbreak, every rising of the city mobs, even for the infrequent air accidents, of that fact I was firmly convinced. But— proof? What man may summon a shadowy feeling to testify in his behalf?

That thought brought curiosity in its wake. Why had Thran of Gorl, whom to my knowledge I had never before set eyes on, come at the exact moment when his speech in my favor could most aid me? I had thought that I was familiar with all the Lords of the Learned Ones, but he was a stranger. And yet a man of his personal magnetism and powers should be widely known. Gorl was a rocky island far to the north; it contained no cities of any importance and its population was mostly made up of needy fishermen. Who was Thran of Gorl?

Intent upon this and other problems, I had wandered deeper into the gardens than I had intended. And now I came upon a wide, smooth lawn of thick yellow moss where were gathered a group of ladies watching the antics of a pair of those tiny creatures called Anas. I would have retreated at once but one of the maids, catching sight of me, called out:

"My Lord, take pity on our plight. San-san's Ana has fled into the bushes and will not come out because these two evil ones have pulled its fur. There it lingers crying. Will you rescue the poor thing for us?"

It was Analia who so called to me, Anatan's younger sister, the daughter of an old and noble military family. Now, at her asking, I dropped my hindering cloak and doffed my helmet before, encouraged by their cries, I pushed into the thick bushes.

The Ana came to me without urging and I brought it out in triumph, my hair sadly ruffled and a couple of long scarlet scratches across my forearm. These Analia was pleased to exclaim over and nothing would do but I must be borne off into a neighboring glade where there was a fountain and my trifling hurts could be looked to.

In their artless company I forgot something of my ever-present worries. I had never really been young or enjoyed the delights of thoughtless youth. On my fifteenth name day I had assumed the place and troubles of a man, and since that day I had never relaxed for a single hour my vigilance against a world which I knew by hard-won experience to be a difficult place in which to exist. But now, for a short half hour, in the company of the court maidens, I recaptured a slender portion of that unexperienced youth.

It was ended all too soon. But I did not begrudge it because of that ending. Through the slender fronds of the fern trees came one I knew well.

Thrala of the Learned Ones stood smiling at us.

Every ripple of her black hair seemed to net itself

about my heart and the wonder of her held me numb. I was content to stand and watch the play of expression on her face as her ladies with cries of joy-filled pleasure gathered about her.

3

The Sotan Pleasure Palace

"Greetings, my Lord Garan." She smiled into my eyes.

"And to you, Flower of Yu-Lac." I touched the hand she held out to me to lips and forehead.

"You have neglected us, my Lord. Do the cares of your office weigh so heavily upon you that you cannot grant us an hour or two of your company?"

I stood agape, unable to summon my wits in quick reply to this gentle mockery. "I am, as always, at your command, royal Lady," I stammered.

"Then you will obey me now," she countered swiftly. "Attend me to the Blue Pool, my Lord. I have need of another pair of hands to aid me there. Nay, little ones, stay you here."

So dismissing her maids she led me away with her. But instead of following the path to the Blue Pool, she sought a tiny rockery and there took her place upon the stone bench.

"Sit down, Garan; I have much to say and little enough time in which to say it. First—let me look at you. How long? Three years, is it not? I can even tell you the number of hours in the days. Why were you not born—? But enough! You have done well for yourself, Garan.''

"Only because—" I began eagerly, but her soft fingers flew to seal my rebellious lips, barring a rush of rash words.

"Not that, Garan, not that! It is of other things we must speak. You seem to have delved in dangerous pools of knowledge, asked awkward questions of the wrong people. And what have you learned?''

I shrugged. "Little enough. Each path ends at last in a black barrier."

She nodded. "Oh, they are clever, clever. But you have made something of a beginning. For that—well, watch behind you of nights, Garan. You walk a rotten bridge; be sure that it does not break to plunge you into a gulf. But from this hour forth you shall not fight alone, soldier. Do you know one Thran of Gorl?''

"I looked upon him for the first time an hour ago."

"Thran, like you, has been laying his ear to the ground and so has heard things not meant for him. Twice has his path of secret watching crossed yours and thus he learned that there was another who mistrusted the future. For all of us, Garan, are not idlers and children playing in the sun. Some of us prepare for the coming storm—''

"Then you have some definite idea of what comes?" I broke in eagerly.

"Not yet. There was a new pleasure palace opened in the Sotan district a week ago.''

I frowned, bewildered by her swift change of subject. "So my aide told me."

"It might be well for you to visit it, Garan.''

"But—" I began a hasty protest.

"Oh, it is well enough known that you enter not into such joys, but allow yourself to be persuaded—tonight. Nay, more I cannot say. Be—careful, Garan. Now go and quickly, before my maids come seeking me. Three years, Garan—" Her soft voice trailed away as she sent me from her. I dared not look back.

In a daze created by my own unleashed emotions, I sought the landing stage and my flier. The black ship from Koom still rested there, aloof and striking among the brightly-colored craft which now thronged the surface of the platform, but I spared it no more than a single passing glance. My thoughts were all for that interview and what might lie hidden within those two words of hers—"three years."

I did not come wholly to myself again until my flier landed upon the stage of the defense tower and I saw Anatan's boyish figure crossing hurriedly toward me. Then I remembered the promise I had so lightly made him that morning. The impossibility had become true.

"Zacat of Ru has come in, my Lord. He is awaiting you in the wardroom," burst out the young officer almost before my feet had touched the floor of the landing stage.

"Bring him to my private rooms at once!" I ordered.

Ru was the northernmost colony of Yu-Lac's glittering chain of dependencies. For three months of the year its wind-harried plains were well-nigh uninhabitable. But wealth lay in its stark mountains for the taking so we held it in a jealous grip. A line of fortified posts, tiny oases of civilization, were the bounds we had laid upon that grim land.

Zacat was an officer of the old school who controlled both men and country with a heavy, but always just, hand. I trusted him above any other of my

under officers. An event serious enough to bring him
to Yu-Lac was grave enough to shadow the future. It
was with a feeling of sudden cold that I paced my
inner chamber awaiting his arrival.

"Hail, Lord." The burly figure in the doorway
drew himself up in formal salute.

"Enter, Zacat. I am glad to clasp your hand again.
But what fortune brings you out of your snow-rimmed
north unheralded?"

"An ill fortune, Garan." He measured me with his
eyes as he replied and then, with an air of relief, he
added, "It is well. You are no city-dwelling lordling
yet. There is no fat, no quivering hand, no murky
eye, to betray you. Are you still the lad who followed me into Ulal in the old days?"

"I have not changed, war dog. Nor, I see, have
you. Give me an open fight and I will be glad—"

"An open fight!" He grimaced. "That is what I
cannot grant you, by the Hair of the Dark One! What
man can battle shadows and win?"

To hear my own thoughts issue from this northern
captain was startling.

"What is happening in Ru?"

"Nothing that I can lay my hand upon or it would
speedily end, you may be sure," he said signifi-
cantly. "But there is a growing uneasiness, whisper-
ings I cannot trace to their source, baseless rumors,
mutinous talk. I tell you frankly, Garan, today I
stand alone in Ru."

"You want help?" I hazarded.

He shook his head. "You should know me better
than that, lad. When was I ever one to run whining to
my masters? Nay, no help in the material sense. But
sometimes two heads upon a problem think better
than one. I want to talk freely to the one man in the
Empire I may fully trust. There is trouble in Ru, and

I cannot smell it out. For the first time my every support has failed me—''

"There you do not suffer alone," I cut in harshly.

"What do you mean?"

"Save for you, Anatan of Hol, and one other"—I thought of her in the garden—"I, too, stand alone today. This morning the Emperor questioned my loyalty."

"What!" He was on his feet, staring at me in outraged amazement.

"It is true. All because, like you, I have tried to sift to its base this mass of intrigue which grows ever heavier throughout Krand. I, too, have been fighting shadows, Zacat."

"So"—he sank down in his seat again—"that is the way of it, eh? Well, lad, it seems to be Ulal over again, but this time we must fight with our wits—not our fists. Let us exchange tale for tale and discover what has been happening these past years since last we stood together."

"Tell me of Ru," I urged him.

He frowned. "It is hard to put into words the feeling which grips me when I go from post to post. On the surface all is well; there is no trouble. The country is at peace with the barbarians; there is no disturbance at the mines. And yet I feel as if I were passing across a bridge, the undersupports of which had been destroyed. The thought haunts me that the heart of this bad business lies naked to the eye if I were only clever enough to find it. It is a demon-conceived business.

"Last month the yield from the Sapit mines was less by ten percent than it should have been. And yet the engineers face me with bland explanations which I have not knowledge enough to question. There have been several hundred suicides within the last three months. The new recruits are in bad condition, mentally, morally, physically. Three beast-men were killed near Headquarters Fort and there is nothing to show how they were able to penetrate so far into the settled lands without being sighted. Unnatural lights have appeared in the sky and twice a dump of highly flammable ore has been set afire by mysterious means. There is a new secret religion being practiced by the mountaineers. Little things all but, taken together, enough to make a man think deep.''

''Whom do you suspect?''

He shrugged and then answered me obliquely. ''There was a man from Koom who made a journey through the mountains.''

''Koom! Ever Koom!'' I brought my fist down on the arm of my chair.

''Aye, ever Koom,'' he echoed me heavily. ''And now, what phantoms do you pursue to no purpose?''

''Bread riots in the province of Kut, due to an unexplained failure of the peestal crop. There was rain in abundance, the soil is the richest in the Empire, but this year the fields were strangely barren. And the Learned Ones did not explain it, at least to me.

''Then there is this new cult of the Wandering Star or some such nonsense. I have had to discipline four of my men for attending its meetings and inciting disturbances afterward. Someone has been smuggling bottles of portucal into the barracks and I have had one man hung for introducing the practice of inhaling the smoke of the rait leaves. You know what that leads to?'' He nodded and I continued: ''Like you, I feel an interest in Koom. So much of a one that I have set certain machinery in motion during the past three months.''

"And the result?" There was eagerness in his demand.

"Exactly nothing. And yet I do not think that the investigators I dispatched there were utter fools."

"Traitors?" he hazarded.

"Perhaps. But what can I do? Within an hour I have been warned to guard my own person. And then this business of finding secret Koomian documents among my records. The Emperor ordered me to produce the man responsible for their being there or answer for the deed myself." I went on to explain to Zacat all that had passed when I stood on trial.

"What do you know of this Thran?" I asked in conclusion.

He shook his head. "Nothing. Gorl is insignificant enough, a fish-smelling outcrop of rock in the upper sea. I was on garrison duty there once shortly after I accepted the brand. There were no Learned Ones there then at any rate. But the Lord of Gorl has interested himself in your affairs to some purpose. I would keep him in mind. Also, what is Kepta doing here? In the past he has had little liking for the company of his caste-fellows."

"When do you return to Ru?" I asked him suddenly.

"Early tomorrow," he replied in some surprise. "Why do you ask?"

I smiled. "Then tonight you shall be the traditional soldier on holiday—"

"What do you mean?" he cut in.

"Tonight we shall visit together a new pleasure palace in the Sotan quarter."

He eyed me with some disgust. "Little did I think that Garan of the Fleet would come to the visiting of pleasure palaces—" he began when I interrupted him.

"We go on a mission. I have reason to believe that

there may be certain interesting facts for a discerning man to discover. You should know me better than to doubt me so completely, Zacat.''

The puckered lines on his forehead smoothed out. ''Three years of absolute power and soft living often change a man to his hurt, lad. I did not want to believe you were what your words stamped you.''

''Then you will come?''

''And gladly. After all''—there was sly humor in his tone—''I am not adverse to seeing the interior of a pleasure palace at another's expense.''

''Good, it is agreed then. And now, what do you say to holding morning inspection with me?''

''Done! That is more to my taste than all the pleasure palaces in this hothouse city of yours.''

So with Anatan and Zacat at my heels I set about my daily rounds. And it seemed to my mind, sharpened as it was by the affair of the morning, that I uncovered enough on that tour to arouse suspicion in the mildest of men. A fraction's delay in carrying out a straight order, a trace of slackness which persisted in spite of my rebukes, a faint beginning of blight upon the crack troops, a certain heady recklessness to be noted in the younger men—I saw it all, and the result brought home to me, as nothing else might, how I, and others like me, stood in the growing shadow of some formless danger.

I knew that Zacat had also seen what lay plain before us and that he too was sifting and weighing impressions gained on the morning tour. We sat together at dinner in the eating hall but there was little talk between us until we had finished and I turned to him.

''Well?''

He shook his head. ''What man can discipline shadows? What I have seen here is but what I face in

Ru. And what advice have I to give when I cannot put my own house in order? But I swear upon the Sword Hand of On Himself, lad, that in this I am with you to the end, be that what it may. Now let us go to this palace of yours, since you are so determined upon it."

We sought my dressing room and there got ourselves into rich but inconspicuous undress uniforms, for I hoped to conceal our identity if I might. Anatan had been warned to do likewise and, after I had fastened a pouch heavy with the bar-like coins of the city to my belt, we found him outside the door, breathing hard through pure excitement.

"Hold in mind," I cautioned him, "that we must remain unknown if possible and tonight we are on duty. Do not allow yourself to be separated from us and, above all, keep a quiet tongue between your teeth."

"To hear is to obey, Lord."

I took one last look about me. Some inner sense must have warned me that it would be long before I returned down that corridor. "Let us go."

On the landing stage a plain flier, unmarked by any betraying insignia, awaited us and we climbed in. Anatan took the controls and we arose in lazy spirals from the military quarter. According to my aide, we must land on the public stage adjoining the palace, as only regular and well-known habitués were allowed the privilege of using the private stage on its roof.

Zacat protested this strongly but my desire for secrecy led me to overrule him, to my regret. A few moments later the violet lamps of the public stage were below us and Anatan set the flier down. The attendant approached to wave us into line with the other ships and accept the fee Anatan had ready for his hand. Zacat and I kept in the background, our helmets pulled far down so that their bird-like beaks overshadowed our faces.

Anatan pouched the receipt for the ship and we sought the ramp which led down to the street level. There, without being noticed, we slipped into the throng. Yu-Lac was always at its best after nightfall. Then did the rhythm of its life grow loud and full, an illusion of carefree gaiety cloaking the idle pastimes of the city dwellers.

"To the right," Anatan guided us.

I literally gasped when I beheld our objective for the first time. Wealth must have been poured forth like water to create the dream which stood before us. The walls, carved with beasts and flowers, were of a creamy crystal faintly flushed with rose which shaded to deep saffron at the foundations.

The broad portal was open according to regulations but a thin shimmering curtain veiled the delights within from the eyes of the casual passerby. On the twelve rose steps leading up to it lounged the body-guards and serving men wearing the liveries of a half dozen or more of the wealthiest lords of the city. All castes save the military were represented.

A slim brown slave girl, with the slanting, provoc-ative eyes of a Teriation, stood waiting to draw the curtain for our passage. She flashed a sly and impish grin at me.

"So you favor us tonight, Lord Garan?"

My faint hope of secrecy was gone.

"Aye, moon-flower. Shall a humble warrior of the Fleet be barred from partaking of your joys?"

"Never!" She laughed strangely. Then, plucking from her girdle one of those flute-like whistles of her native desert land, she blew a low sweet note.

A slender white hand slipped through the curtain and beckoned us within. The Teriation smiled.

"The guide awaits you, my Lord. Enter."

With my two companions I passed through the slit in the curtain.

4

Ila and Lania

The square entrance hall in which we found ourselves was lighted with a mellow yellow glow from one of the new sun lamps. A broad archway, veiled in purple shot with metallic green, faced us. With hand upon the folds of this curtain stood our waiting guide, a maid from the ice-bound shores of Northern Ahol. Her slight limbs were swathed in amber silk and wide bands of soft copper confined her breast and waist. The artfully tangled mass of her red-gold hair concealed all but a thin white wedge of her face.

At our entrance she sank forward to her knees and touched her hands, palm down, to the pavement. "Will the noble Lords be pleased to follow me?" Her voice was thin but shrilly sweet.

Zacat plucked at my arm. "They seem to take too much pleasure in our company, lad. I feel as if we were walking into the mouth of a sapt cage."

I pressed his fingers in warning. But I too felt a tingle awaken my flesh. His illustration was apt. Only three days before had I witnessed a worn-out and aged grippon being coaxed along the ramp which led to the cage of a giant sapt. And he had gone willingly enough to his end, trusting the men who urged him on.

The girl held back the curtain. Without hesitation I entered.

Like a golden bowl, carved to meet the lips of some mountain godling, was the room in which we found ourselves. It was oval in shape, ringed by twenty archways like the one through which we had come, each curtained by a sheet of bewildering and melting color. Overhead the walls domed sharply into a cone, the point of which was open to the stars.

From where we stood the floor sank down, by a series of wide steps completely encircling the room. In the center of this nest of ever-narrowing rings was a shallow oval pit from which arose lazy strings of colored, scented vapor. The massive steps were crowded with heaps of priceless metallic fabrics, flagons of gem-set stone, tiny tables heaped with dainties. And here lounged most of those who had preceded us, ministered to by the beauties of the palace.

And they were beautiful. Never before had I seen all the race types produced beneath Krand's sun assembled together, each startling in her loveliness. Like the brown-skinned Teriation at the outer door and the white Aholian at my side, each was a perfect specimen of her race.

I heard Anatan draw a deep breath and Zacat chuckle.

"A pleasure to loot, this place," the latter observed dryly. "It is not hard to understand why these palaces are barred to those below the rank of wing officer. A few of my Ruian lads in here—"

"By the Breath of Zant," broke in Anatan, "look to that maid in black. Have you ever seen her like?"

He pointed to one of the Lapidian cave dwellers. Her

hair, bleached to bone whiteness by the generations her people have dwelt away from the light, was wreathed around her proud head in heavy coils. From throat to heel she was wrapped in dead black, but her white arms were naked to the shoulder. She was a striking and outstanding figure as she moved slowly through the ranks of her more brightly-robed companions.

"Would you linger here, my Lords? Or are you for the inner courts, perhaps?" the Aholian asked softly when we had looked our fill.

"The inner courts," I answered quickly before Anatan could protest.

We followed her around the uppermost step from which opened the twenty curtained archways. Anatan tugged at my cloak, whispering: "Ask to see the Lady of the Palace. It is customary to do so upon the first visit."

Wondering where he had gained his knowledge, I obeyed his instructions. The Aholian nodded and immediately pulled aside a flame and silver hanging at another door. Many were the wonders through which we passed. I remember one room that was walled with transparent crystal behind which swam living monsters from the outer seas, queer things with phosphorescent bodies or jaws gleaming in the dim light. And there were other chambers as strange or as weirdly beautiful.

Then at length we came into a small room, white-walled and floored. But the dome was lacquered night-black, studded with great stars of crystal. Here on a couch of vivid scarlet rested the one who was ruler of all this maze of color.

By her dress and heavily painted face she was a woman of Arct. In contrast to her maids outside she was hideously plain. Thin to the point of emaciation, her sheath-like covering of silver net revealed every bone and hollow. Her face was thickly enameled after the fashion of her country, huge purple circles about her sunken eyes, orange slashes for lips and the rest flat white.

But her glorious hair was her claim to a place in that palace of charm. Black and very long, it was undisfigured by any fastenings or pins, rippling in freedom down to lie upon the floor when she was seated.

However, it was not at the ruler of the pleasure palace that I stared open-mouthed in amazement, but at the man who lolled, thick-tongued and sprawling at her feet. Thran of Gorl, a two-handled wine cup in his unsteady hands, leered at me. Dragging upon her couch for support, he rose waveringly to his feet.

"Other friends of yours, Ila? But then I cannot complain if others seek your company, can I? Your sweetness is not mine alone, alas. But may I stay a while or must I go?"

She shook her head and the eyes she turned upon us were chill with unfriendliness. "Stay, my Lord. As for you, my Lord strangers, I bid you welcome to my domain. But whisper your desires into Lania's ears and what you wish shall be set before you." She motioned toward the Aholian. So negligently did she dismiss us.

Thran laughed jeeringly and swayed toward me. "This sweet is not for your plucking, soldier. Go search other gardens for your spoil."

Something clicked faintly against the throat buckle of my cloak and fell down into the folds of my sash. Playing the abashed boor, I edged myself and my companions out of the chamber, leaving Ila and her lordling to the solitude they so desired.

My fingers touched Anatan's shoulder and I put my lips close to his ear.

"You amuse this Lania for the moment."

He glanced at me quickly and then slipped forward to keep pace with the glide of the Aholian handmaid. I fumbled in my sash and drew forth an oval silver bead the size of my thumb. A moment's inspection under the direct rays of one of the corridor lights revealed the faint line of cleavage about its middle. I was familiar enough with such devices for the safe-keeping of secret messages. A single twirl of my fingers separated it into halves and then I was unrolling a bit of writing silk. It read:

In the Room of the Grippons. One hour from now. Trust no one here.

In silence I passed the note to Zacat. He scanned the single line and then grinned wolfishly. "We seem to have bayed upon a hot scent after all, Garan. The Room of the Grippons it is. Now it lies with us to play the roisters. Your boy Anatan will aid us there."

It gave me a twinge of uneasiness when I looked up to see Anatan's dark head so close to the golden one of the Aholian. For it was plain to the most stupid beholder that they had reached some understanding and were embarking upon a flirtation. The boy must be warned not to play the fool now.

I quickened my steps and came up to them. By displaying the manners of a pothouse bully I shouldered Anatan away and hailed his companion brusquely. "How now, mistress. We have paid our duty to your lady, now lead us to your haven of joys. Set your wonders before us."

Anatan was about to protest my unseemly behavior when, using a fold of my cloak as a blind, I thrust Thran's message into his hand. A tug at my back informed me that he had read and understood.

"What would you, my Lords?" asked Lania, sweetly submissive. "Wines? We have the best. Heady white vintages of Ru, rich purple streams from Hol, golden from Koom—and others in abundance. Dancers to amuse you? In one of our halls the golden maids from the forbidden temples of Qur tread the mystic mazes of the olden gods, the like to be seen nowhere else in all Yu-Lac. Or do you wish companions for the evening? A girl from the deserts of Teriatia, as hard to withstand as one of her country's fierce winds, a Lapidian of the silver hair and passionate lips, a woman of Arct with all the pleasing city vices at her command? All nations, all natures have we here.''

"The temple dancers," selected Zacat quickly and I applauded his choice for, of the three Lania had given us, that seemed the least likely to involve us in future difficulties.

Without a word she turned into a cross corridor which soon became a ramp leading downward. Then for the first time I saw a shade of uneasiness cloud Zacat's face. Anatan was definitely sober and walked a little behind, as if he had his doubts of our enterprise. At the time I believed him sulking, but later I learned that he had good reason to distrust our hasty choice of evening entertainment. Hol borders the tropic jungle land of Qur and he suspected what lay at the foot of that ill-omened ramp.

Although Krand was united in the worship of On and had been so united for centuries, yet there still persisted in such primitive nations as Qur and Ru temples to the olden gods, those dark entities our people worshiped before they dragged themselves up out of the pit of the beast. I, myself, knew very little concerning these forbidden and now secret practices; in fact, few but the adepts did. And of those adepts Qur was the last stronghold.

A thin piping, so high in scale that our human ears could barely distinguish its notes, broke the silence.

And with that piping came a low throbbing, as if air, dead and heavy with the weight of untold years, were pulsing out the measure of some unhuman rhythm.

Zacat hesitated suddenly, shuffling his feet and changing step. "Rhythm—hypnotic control," he murmured. "Do not surrender to it."

Anatan, too, was constantly changing step, from stride to shuffle and back. Clumsily I began to follow their example. The ramp seemed to run down into the depths of Krand itself and there was no break in its smooth polished walls. The ever-glowing lights, placed at intervals in the roof above our heads, changed gradually in shade from warm gold to icy blue and then to a sort of misty gray. But still the strange shrill piping and the deep throbbing marked the measure of our steps while we hopped and shuffled to escape its binding spell. But Lania went onward unconcerned, without a backward glance.

At last we came out into a sort of anteroom floored and walled with dull gray. Lania lifted up her high voice in a wailing cry and at once a section of the wall moved inward exposing the darkness beyond.

"A precaution we must take." Lania nodded toward the secret door. "Some of our enchantments are not for common eyes."

Through the slit-like door the weird music came louder, sounds which seemed to have some strange life and being of their own. The Aholian passed within and we followed, but Zacat, always quick of wit, snapped loose his sheathed sword and placed it in the crack of the door so that it remained open a good two inches.

We were in utter blackness, a darkness so thick that it seemed a tangible veil. A hand touched mine and my fingers closed about Anatan's gemmed wristlet. A moment later I heard Zacat's heavy breathing at my right.

"Wait and watch, soldiers." There was faint subtle mockery in Lania's voice.

The strange and broken rhythm was growing louder, menacing. "Move your fingers, your hands, in opposition to it," whispered Anatan. I felt his wrist twist free from my grasp. Obediently I strove to carry out his suggestion.

Then, out of the darkness above us, came a single ray of light, green and yet gray. A light which seemed the corrupting emanation of something vilely and anciently dead. There was a scheming wary evil in that light. As we watched it, fascinated, winged shapes of gold swam into and through it, circling ever downward until at last they touched a black pavement, the blocks of which might have been hewn in the quarries of that Elder Race, they who held Krand before human foot touched its surface.

The great golden wings drooped, closed, and were gone as if their wearers no longer had any use for them. Then the fifteen shapes of living yellow began their dance. Wild and beautiful, yet full of an age-old meaning which was utterly evil, was that dance. Each pose of seductive invitation, each gliding step, seemed aimed to draw out of the depths of the watcher that darker part of him which is his heritage from the beasts.

When I sensed this, I fought with every ounce of strength within me to master those far in-dwelling thoughts and passions which the dancers recalled with their weaving spell. Before me I saw again the blood-drenched streets of Ulal when we sacked it, and all that chanced therein when, drunk with bloodlust, we poured into the city which had withstood our might for so long. And there were things done that day—

I clutched in the dark at my companions. "Come, let us out of here!" I cried. I felt them awaken under my hands as if they were shaking themselves free of some numbing dream. And then we turned and fled from the sight of those golden dancers and the evil web they were weaving about us.

Setting our fingers in the crack of the hidden door we tore it open. Zacat retrieved his sword and then we were on the ramp, eyes strained and staring, hearts pounding as if we were engaged in a race which was taxing us to the very limit of our strength. We were halfway up when an amber shadow joined us.

"The dancers are strong meat, soldiers." Again mockery overlay Lania's tones. "Too strong for you, it seems."

I rounded on her, half in earnest, half playing the role I had set myself. "Give us no more of your devilish mysteries. We wish human pleasures, not those subscribed to by night demons!"

"To hear is to obey, Lord. What do you say to a quiet supper in a private room—with suitable companions in attendance?"

"That will do, mistress," Zacat growled acceptance.

With the air of knowing well how to please us, she led the way through a maze of turning, twisting corridors and elaborate chambers until we came into a small, but fanciful, room done in steely blue. Four life-sized figures quartered the hemisphere that was dome and wall. Great, gray grippons they were, rearing as though in anger.

I did not need Zacat's sudden grip upon my arm to tell me where I was. We stood in the room Thran had appointed for our meeting place.

There was a low divan at the far end of the chamber and there Lania bid us seat ourselves while she went to give orders for our serving. But as she was going she looked full into my face.

"The room pleases you, Lord?"

"Well enough," I answered shortly.

To my utter amazement she laughed and flung back her head, so that for the first time we saw clearly the face beneath her tangled mass of copper curls. Anatan rose to his feet with a sharp cry of mixed discovery and chagrin.

"Analia!"

"Even so, brother." Again she laughed. Then, going to our right, she twitched the curtain hanging there. Thran stepped forth, all signs of drunkenness gone from him, again the keen, masterful figure I had seen that morning in the Hall of the Nine Princes.

And he led Ila by the hand, but now there was a subtle difference in her bearing as if beneath her paint lay hidden another identity.

"Do you not know me, Lord Garan?" she asked softly.

And immediately I was on my knees, staring open-mouthed into that hideously defiled face, for it was my Lady Thrala who stood there, disguised beneath the paint and garish robes of the women of Arct.

She turned to Thran with a smile. "We are better mummers than we had thought, my Lord. Nay, Garan, I am not the Ila you saw before. Ila and Lania are—elsewhere for this hour. We take their places. The real Ila is somewhat different—"

"Which is not surprising," observed Thran dryly, "since she is a creature of Kepta's. Now let us get down to business. The hours fly only too swiftly when danger spins the world."

5

The Taking of Thrala

"Is it altogether wise to speak here?" demanded Zacat bluntly. "Walls of pleasure palaces are reputed to possess more than one set of ears."

"Not here. This room is safe. Ila and Kepta have seen to that, for it serves their purposes at times," answered Thran. "And what has happened to the Lord of Ru that he has developed so suspicious a mind?"

"Naught—that I can lay hand to," he growled.

"Naught that you can lay hand to. That may be well said of all of us. And yet for two years you, Lord Garan, have pried and spied in closed ways. Even in distant Gorl there has been uneasiness in the air. Nor are we wrong, any of us"—his voice rose triumphantly—"for this very place wherein we sit gives lie to the confident peace of our world. Do you know who is behind Ila, who so subtly planned each soul-tarnishing joy of this muckheap? Kepta, the Koomian! He, who this very morning attempted to involve you with the council, Lord Garan, and so rid himself of one who was beginning to suspect too much.

"That night-demon Ila is his match for twisted wits and this whole wonder box her trap to capture those Kepta wishes, Kanddon of Stal, Palkun, and all the rest. And who are we who are not yet blinded, who can still see clearly enough to turn aside from Kepta and all his works? A handful against a world. Some twenty of my caste, the Lord of Ru, you and your young aide here. And whom can you lean upon?"

"Frankly no one except those you have named. My entire corps is pervaded by a taint to which I can lay no name. In my mind the whole of Yu-Lac is rotted by some vile distemper."

"For Yu-Lac substitute Krand and you will be nearer the truth. Kepta has built better than even he guesses. For, if he knew his power, we would all suddenly cease to be. To be plain, Kepta has been an earnest seeker after what we know as the 'Dark Knowledge' and he is very pleased with the powers which have answered his summoning, so pleased that he wishes to make all Krand partake of his joy."

"We have been at fault, we Learned Ones," broke in Thrala. "Too long have we drifted, losing interest in everything but the depths of our own learning. Had we been alert, sentries against the forces of the Outer Dark as we were in the older days, this evil would not have come among us. Would See-leen, the founder of our race, have suffered Kepta to live one hour beyond the discovery of his practices?"

"You forget"—there was sadness in Thran's rich voice—"See-leen headed a united people. What army follows us? Nay, we must fight alone, perhaps a losing fight."

"And how do you propose we fight?" Zacat cut

in. "By force of arms? I think Kepta has more potent weapons."

"Just so. Therefore we must penetrate his defenses by guile, for, before we lay our plans, we must know the purpose and place of his attack. One of us must enter Koom."

"Impossible," I said curtly.

"Why?"

"Do you think that I haven't tried it?" I rounded on him. Learned or no, I knew my duty and had always performed it to the best of my ability. "When I took leave three months ago I made a personal attempt. I returned no wiser. With this—" I unbuckled my war cloak and pulled it away from my throat to expose a thin blue scar line. "That was to be a death blow."

"So." Thran eyed me intently. "I did not know of that."

"Nor anyone else until now. What man is proud of failure?"

"But our problem remains," said the Gorlian.

Thrala shook her head. "To the contrary, it is solved."

"What do you mean?"

"That I shall go to Koom. Kepta will not suspect me. Why should he? Have I not kept apart from all laboratory work, shown no interest in knowledge seeking, so that even my father thinks me a discredit to our caste? I will go to Koom for a pleasant adventure and its Master will suspect nothing."

"Nay!" The word burst from between my lips with the force of a sword thrust. "You cannot do it! If what I suspect of Koom is true, no clean living mortal dares to venture there and hope to come forth again unbesmirched. Kepta plays with pitch."

"And who is Lord Garan to say me aye or nay?"

Surely then, in that one wild moment, I must have revealed my jealously guarded secret for all the world to gape at.

"The humblest of your many servants, Royal Lady. Yet even I dare to say no to your will in this matter."

"He is right enough," agreed Zacat heavily. "Koom is no place for a woman."

Thran nodded in agreement. But Thrala was unconvinced. What further arguments she would have brought forward to bolster up her plan, we never knew, for suddenly from the domed roof above us came the soft tones of a chime. Thran and Thrala froze and then looked at each other with eyes in which excitement burned like a flame.

"That is a warning," said the Gorlian. "Someone is coming along the passage. We must go."

"The inner corridor," suggested Thrala. "Show them, Thran."

He arose and stepped to the curtain from behind which he and Thrala had entered. The bare wall split into halves, revealing a narrow door through which we squeezed, one by one.

"You get through, Thran," whispered Thrala. "Remember, a woman's voice alone closes this portal."

Obediently he joined us in the corridor beyond but the Lady Thrala did not follow. Instead the halves came to with a snap, and we were left bewildered in the dark. Thran flung himself at that blank wall.

"It's the rankest folly!" he stormed. "She cannot play Ila well enough to deceive any of that woman's intimates."

At his words I comprehended for the first time the trick Thrala had played upon us. Having rid the room of us, she was about to face the newcomer, whomever he might be. My shoulder was beside Thran's in a futile attack upon that stubborn door.

Someone dug fiercely at my back with long nails. "Let be!" It was Analia screaming in my ear. "This door opens at the sound of a voice alone. Let me try."

Accordingly, Thran and I stepped back, granting her the position she demanded. We kept silent while she repeated some formula in the high, shrill voice that was Lania's.

A dark crack appeared lengthwise and with its coming we could both see and hear what passed in the Chamber of the Grippons. I, for one, was not surprised to see Kepta's dark handsome face with its faintly sneering smile. But behind him stood another. Thran clutched my arm.

"Ila!"

The real Ila it was, the Ila of the white and black chamber, with her starved body and glorious hair, her painted face and her spite-filled voice. Facing her, proudly erect, was Thrala. Two Ilas, yet how different.

"—an unexpected pleasure," Kepta's smooth tones ran on. "The Lady Ila is honored that you should find pleasure in wearing the type of dress she has introduced to Yu-Lac. Yet I fear that we must be rude enough to ask the cause of this delightful meeting—"

Ila put an end to his baiting of Thrala, for she had seen the telltale billowing of the curtain across the secret door where we crouched. These tapestries had been woven so that they were transparent to those behind them but solid to those within the room.

"Fool!" she spat at Kepta. "She is not alone. Get her away—"

At that I ripped aside the curtain and sprang

forward, sword in hand, but I was too late. For Kepta, with the quickness of one of those tree reptiles which inhabit the forests of Qur, jerked Thrala toward him and thrust her fighting form into Ila's merciless arms. He met my attack by spinning the divan across my path.

I went down, cursing, and a moment later Thran and Zacat were on me. But I caught a glimpse of Anatan hurtling our bodies and now but two paces behind the Koomian.

Raging savagely I gained my feet. Zacat, bellowing vengeance, was already off and I was not far behind him. But we had not far to go, for rounding a turn in the corridor we came upon Anatan beating furiously at the wall with fist and sword hilt.

"They passed through here!" he cried as we came up to him.

But on the smooth curve of the wall there was no mark of door. There Thran and Analia found us baffled. The Learned One had mastered his rage.

"They have fled to Koom," he announced with finality. "Only in Koom will they be safe, for they know all Yu-Lac will be aroused against them."

"Koom it is." I admitted the force of his argument. "It is well that—"

I turned when he caught my wrists. "Where are you going?"

"To Koom."

"How?"

"I have a flier—"

He interrupted at once. "They would bring you down within six miles of their sea wall. There is another way."

"And that?"

"Through that place where you saw the dancers of Qur. That hall is part of the ancient Ways of Dark-

ness, the corridors hollowed out beneath the shell of
Krand by those entities who labored here before man
came to rule. The way to Koom is there for that man
who dares to take it.''

"I dare any road," I returned hotly.

Zacat showed his yellow teeth. "With good steel
in hand a man may pick and choose his road. When
do we start?''

Thran drew a sheaf of writing leaves from his belt
pouch and held them out to me. "Make out a request
for instant leave for you and Zacat—''

"Anatan also!" cried the boy. "Nay," he added,
seeing dissent in my face, "I will go if I must follow
after in your tracks.''

"For the three of you then. I will see that it
reaches the proper authorities. We must have provisions and weapons—''

Zacat touched his sword but Thran shook his head.

"Some of the dangers we must face, if legend
speaks true, are to be met with something more
potent than steel.''

"So?" I broke in. "Well, the resources of my
office lie open to us. Give me half an hour within the
great armory and I swear I can provide us with the
means of leveling all Koom to dust.''

It was Analia who made the decision for us. "Let
Lord Garan return to his armory and get the weapons
he has spoken of. I will see him through the private
ways. And an hour before dawn we will meet in the
tenth court. You go with Lord Garan, Anatan.''

"An hour before dawn? So long?" I demanded,
ever seeing Thrala struggling in the bony arms of that
she-demon and Kepta's slow smile hinting of name-
less evils. To go about calmly, collecting weapons,
provisions— Every throbbing nerve within me rebelled
wildly. I wished to rush in upon the Master of Koom,

to slay and slay until the red blood bubbled across the floor. The knowledge that Koom lay a hundred air miles off our coast, and that it would be longer by the Ways, did nothing to temper my impatience.

"He dare not harm her," Thran said quietly. "Nor would he if he could."

"You mean?"

"Today he asked the Emperor for Thrala as his mate."

My fingers curled as if to seek a shadowy throat. Never had my hatred of Kepta been so intense. That creeper in the dark to aspire to—her! I smiled and saw Analia shrink from that smile.

"Another score between us," I muttered and then added aloud, "Of your kindness, show me these private ways of yours, mistress. The sooner I am about my business, the sooner we can march upon the spoor of this hunter of the Pit."

"An hour before dawn in the tenth court," Thran reminded us.

I nodded curtly and, with Anatan, followed the quick-witted Analia from the room. By diverse winding, hidden ways hollowed in the walls, we stumbled after her. I learned later that from the first those three, Thran, Thrala, and Analia, had watched the building of the pleasure palace, having guessed its purpose. The master designer of its wonders had parted with his own set of plans for a price. Plans wherein each secret lay plainly marked. For whole days and nights at a time since its opening, Thrala and Analia had played their parts within its walls, coming and going with ease through passages that Kepta and Ila thought known only to themselves.

We came out at last into a narrow alley, ill-lit and deserted.

"Mark this place well," Analia bade us as she let

us out. "When you return here, tap three times with your sword hilt. Now go quickly before you are sighted."

Once out of that dark lane Anatan had little difficulty in finding the way to the public landing stage where we had left the flier. We had little time, for already the city was quieting down for the few hours of slumber before sunrise. I was, I will admit, taking small notice of the street along which we hurried, for my thoughts were intent upon the contents of my military storehouse and I was mentally listing those weapons and accouterments which would prove of greatest service to us.

Thus it happened that the first warning I had of trouble was when a raving, slavering something charged at me out of an opening between two buildings. I strove to draw my sword, but abandoned the effort at once. There was no time for steel.

I caught a fleeting glimpse of my attacker before he closed with me. His features were set in the horrible rigidity of the rait user. Foam dribbled from his cracked lips. His crooked fingers were extended ready to dig at my eyes, a favorite form of attack of those whom rait turns into beasts. And, to my added horror, I saw that he wore the trappings of an under officer in my own force.

My startled cry and the shrieks of my attacker brought Anatan around too late. Fast clasped as I was in the fellow's grip, he dared not strike for fear of wounding me.

I braced myself against the shock of meeting and managed to get in a sharp blow upon the side of his throat just before his stubby fingers dug and tore at the flesh of my neck above the edge of my corselet. It was that one blow which must have saved me, for it landed, more by the luck of fate than by any intention of mine, upon a nerve and so momentarily checked him.

With a crash of body armor we landed on the pavement, my attacker still tearing at my throat, while I, wriggling like a serpent of the outer sea, strove to free myself from his hold. With a snap his stained teeth came together a scant half inch from my flesh and I realized with a mixture of fear and horror that I was struggling in the hands of one of those unfortunates whom rait turns into carnivorous hunters. I was only meat to appease his ravenous and unnatural hunger.

Now freed from the first shock of surprise, I caught his wrists in one of those holds taught by the Lapidians, by which they can force a man to break his own bones. The thing astride me howled and snapped again, this time grazing my skin.

I bore down upon his wrists and then his teeth closed upon my left hand, piercing it to the bone. By the Grace of On, I managed to hold my grip long enough for Anatan to come to my rescue. With all his force he brought the heavy pommel of his dress sword down upon the rait smoker's unprotected head.

The man blinked and sighed, then rolled away from me. I was able to scramble up unsteadily. Blood dripped from my wounded hand to splatter on the pavement. But to my utter amazement we were alone. The noise of our fight and the cries of my attacker had brought no one. I looked about the deserted street and then at Anatan. He nodded soberly and I knew that the same thought which whirled through my dizzy head occupied him also. We had been set upon by design.

Someone had laid a trap and we had walked heavy-footed into it. The rait smoker had been placed there for our disadvantage.

"Let him lie." Anatan jerked his head toward the limp body of my late opponent. "We had better reach the flier while we are still able."

Agreeing heartily, I twisted the corner of my cloak about my bloody hand and we took to our heels in earnest. Though we passed into more brilliantly-lighted and well-peopled avenues we did not slacken our pace. Shortly we were panting up the ramp to the landing stage.

There we must wait while the sleepy attendant brought out our flier. And I, for one, did not breathe freely again until we were both within the narrow confines of its closed cabin.

"Make for the armory," I directed Anatan, "and land on its roof. I shall take no more chances this night. When we return, try to make a landing within that alley."

"Difficult business," he commented.

"But better than another meeting with a rait smoker. And it can be done by a careful man."

A second later our landing gear touched upon the flat roof of the squat armory wherein were kept the secrets of my force for the protection of all Yu-Lac.

6

The Ways of Darkness

By the mist of light from the tiny radium rod I carried in my belt pouch I located the trap door covering the ramp which led from the roof. Around my neck night and day I wore the key which unlocked this and every other door within the confines of the military quarter. I now put this to use.

But it required Anatan's strength as well as mine to raise that ponderous slab of metal-bound stone and lay it back upon the roof. Again my radium rod came into use, lighting the thick dark below us.

Having in mind just which storerooms I wished to plunder, I sped down the ramp and through the maze of narrow corridors it gave upon, until, at last, I came to a door marked with a broad scarlet strip. I unlocked this, my fingers trembling so that the key clinked against the lock plate, for I firmly believed that I was running a race with time itself.

Within, neatly laid up in glass-fronted bins, were suits of scales made to cover a man from head to foot, even to his fingertips. They were light in weight but chemically treated so as to withstand all known death vapors and heat rays. Pointing these out to Anatan I gave him his orders.

"Sort out enough of these for all of us. I will join you later on the roof."

Leaving him there, I went down yet another ramp to the floor below, there seeking out the room wherein were stored certain new ray throwers of a radical type not yet issued to the corps. On the testing field they had made an excellent showing in both accuracy and range, but as yet their worth had not been proven to the full satisfaction of our experts.

I laid aside six of these small torch-like rods and with them extra charges of green, violet, and infrared lenses. To the new and untried weapons I added an equal number of the regular pattern in use, again with extra charges. And then, as I turned to go, I came upon a belt of grippon hide equipped with a large radium light cell, the sort of accouterment worn by those venturing into the Lapidian caves. I added this to my spoil.

Back again on the roof I found Anatan, there before me, impatiently pacing about the flier. Besides the indestructible scale suits he had found four war swords of the ancient pattern, swords that were meant to be used in hand-to-hand combat on the field and not as dress ornaments.

We replaced the trap door and I locked it. Then back in the flier Anatan pressed the lever which sent us soaring upward. Avoiding the patrols, flying their regular beats above the city, we circled back over the route we had come.

Luckily the pleasure palace was easy to identify from the air and Anatan speedily discovered our alley. Then, in spite of his doubts, he accomplished an expert piece of maneuvering, setting us down upon its pavement not ten paces from the door. If we had not been in one of the smallest of private ships he could not have done it. As it was there were but two hands' breadth between its polished sides and the alley wall.

We gathered up our spoil and, so laden, went to the door. At my knock it opened smoothly without sound and Analia peered out, bright gleam of her dress and ornaments dulled by the shadows.

Again we traversed those crooked ways within the walls until we stepped through an opening into a small, bare court. There were Thran and Zacat crouched above a tattered strip of yellowed fish skin, the substance upon which the ancients of our race had recorded their deeds.

"You return so soon? That is able work, Lord Garan. Now what do you bring us?"

I hurriedly explained my choice of weapons and held forth one of the scale suits for Thran to examine. In the light the crystalline, octagonal scale possessed a jewel-like sparkle. Zacat smoothed it with all the love of a fighting man for a good tool of his trade. But his interest was thoroughly aroused when Anatan produced the antique war swords.

"Good steel." He ran his thumb down the shining blade of one. "I would rather have this than all the ray rods in Krand. For steel never plays a man false. That is a clever lad, that Anatan of yours."

"It seems that you have robbed your armory to some purpose," agreed Thran, checking our spoils for the second time. "Nor have we been altogether idle while you were gone."

He waved his hand toward a corner of the court and there were heaped small concentrate food containers and jars of the so-called "water" drops which are issued on the march through desert countries. So treated, enough food and water to suffice a man for days might be carried in a belt pouch no larger than my two fists. In addition there was the map over which they had been stooping when we entered.

"Little enough do we know of the underground ways. Save for the perverted Lapidians, we humans have shunned the surface paths below," Thran pointed out as he smoothed his map. "But always there are those who seek knowledge in strange places. Such was the soldier Kem-mec, who lived in Yu-Lac some five thousand years ago.

"They were excavating then for the foundations of the first of the great defense towers and, in order to provide it with an indestructible base, the builders went far deeper below the surface than they had ever pierced before. On the twenty-seventh day of excavation they laid open a section of one of the Ways of Darkness.

"Kem-mec sought and obtained permission to enter and explore the unknown passage in view of its possible future use for military purposes. He was unable to gather any followers and went alone. The equipment of that day was, of course, vastly inferior to that our underground explorers rely upon today, but he did manage to explore and map a large section of the Ways honeycombing the rock upon which Yu-Lac stands. There were abundant indications that these huge tunnels and chambers had been hollowed out by mechanical means and it is supposed that they were the products of the skill of that inhuman race which preceded us in the mastery of this planet.

"His first trip below merely aroused Kem-mec's thirst for further knowledge. He went again and again and finally failed to return. In the meantime it was considered best by Amest the Great, Emperor of Yu-Lac at the time, to close the opening.

"He made this decision suddenly after receiving the confidential report made by Kem-mec upon his return from his next to last trip. It can be readily surmised that the soldier-explorer had discovered something highly dangerous to the city. What it was was never made public.

"Up until half a year ago all Kem-mec's earlier reports and maps moldered undisturbed in the library of the Learned Ones at Semt. But when I wished to look through them, moved by curiosity, I discovered them gone, with the exception of this single map which had been caught against the upper cover of the coffer in which they had been kept. The attendant informed me that Kepta of Koom had, with the permission of the head librarian, withdrawn them for private study.

"Then this place was built and a passage delved to intercept one of the Ways Kem-mec had mapped. At the same time Kepta developed a sudden interest in the age-old temples of Qur, paying them several semi-secret visits. And Qur is, as we know, the last stronghold of that weird faith distilled from the forgotten rites of the Older Ones.

"In leaving me this one map, however, Kepta left a potent weapon. For this traces what we need most now, a route under the sea to Koom. And tradition has it that it was over this route Kem-mec went on that last journey from which he never returned. The fate which overtook Kem-mec five thousand years ago may still await those who follow in his steps today. But it was this path that Kepta and Ila took this night, of that I am certain. Somewhere along its length may lie the menace which caused Amest to seal the Ways. Does that menace still exist?"

Zacat snorted. "We can only go and see."

I was already laying out the scale suits and portioning the weapons. Thran laughed. "It seems that Kem-mec's kind have not deserted his calling. Let us prepare then."

We shed our dress armor and undertunics, then pulled on the tight-fitting scale suits. The basic material, upon which the protecting scales had been laid, had elastic properties which made it cling to the skin of the wearer. A grotesque mask equipped with oaxlenses, which had the power of magnifying distant objects and also enabled those who used them to see clearly in all but absolute darkness, hung down across our shoulders ready to be pulled on.

Once so encased, we were, as far as I knew, invulnerable to any known weapon. The smooth surface of the scales would dull and turn the sharpest blade and withstand as well burning or freezing rays.

Over the scale suits we girded the swords Anatan had brought, hooking to their belts in addition both an old and a new type ray rod. Extra charges for our rods and the small cans of supplies went into pouches of grippon hide, to be carried slung over our backs.

But when we were ready and turned to the door a fifth reptilian figure was awaiting us. Analia, her red wig gone and her dark hair loose about her throat, was engaged in locking about her waist the radium cell belt. To this she calmly proceeded to hook ray rods before stooping to pick up a bag of supplies.

"Analia!" cried her brother. "What madness—?"

"I go," she interrupted him calmly. "Where Thrala has been, there I will follow. And you cannot deny me. I enter this venture with open eyes, even as I have done from the first. And the Ways of Darkness can hold no more danger than this palace has in the past. I go."

And with that she turned and vanished through the door. I turned to Thran, who was folding the remaining scale dress, Anatan having brought six for some reason, into as small a package as he might before slipping it into his supply pouch. He looked up at me with a trace of smile.

"When a woman speaks with that voice, Lord Garan, it is best to allow her her own way at once, for years of argument will not bring her to your way of thinking. Analia will not delay us; she has proved her strength and courage in her mistress' service many times in the past. She goes."

So I was forced to leave it, but the thought of a woman sharing the perils of the unknown was certainly not to my liking. And my resentment was shared by Anatan, who was enraged. Only Zacat cared nothing, being eager to test the dangers of the path before us.

Analia was waiting for us in the hall and under her expert guidance we threaded the web of corridors and chambers in search of that ramp up which we had charged such a short, and yet such a long time ago. In spite of my unspoken doubts we attracted no attention in any of the rooms through which we passed. Our strange dress marked us as entertainers of some sort to the few half-drunken fools we did encounter.

Once again we found and descended the broad ramp, but this time there came no suggestive piping rhythm to entangle our feet and minds, only a dry and dusty silence such as is found in the primeval mountain temples of Ru, a silence full of the dust of vanished centuries. Now the lights did not change color, only grew paler as we advanced, until at last they faded away altogether and we halted to adjust our masks with their darkness-piercing eye shields.

The black pavement was again underfoot but now no corruption-filled ray came from above and the winged, dancing shapes were gone. Here Thran took the lead, hurrying us forward across the vast emptiness of that deserted hall.

Another ramp, this one so steep that we must clutch a handrail of time-smoothed stone, opened before us and, without hesitation, Thran darted down it. Halfway down he sank to his knees and picked up some object which he held out to us. On the palm of his scale glove twinkled a scrap of the glittering stuff which had embellished the robes of Thrala and Ila.

"We follow the right road as this messenger tells us," he said and tossed the scrap away. But I stooped and searched for it, tucking it into my pouch.

Down and down into an ever-thickening darkness we went, darkness which might have overpowered us entirely had it not been for our oax-lenses. Analia would have switched on her radium cell lamp, not knowing what, or who, might lie in wait for us below, but Thran would not allow it. As long as we could see at all it was better not to give warning of our approach.

Now I noted a sudden change in the character of the walls. Before they had been of smooth glistening stone, but now they were of great blocks of some gray substance which had a faintly unpleasant sheen as if coated with thin slime. Thran nodded toward them.

"We are entering the Ways. No one who has ever seen the handiwork of the Older Ones can mistake it."

On and on went the ramp, growing ever steeper so that we were forced to break somewhat our headlong pace and keep a tight hold on the supporting rail. I was wondering apprehensively if it might not become too steep for our footing when it suddenly gave way to a deep trough-like path running almost level into the dense dark before us. As I stepped out upon that weird roadway I felt that those who had constructed that avenue for their own forgotten purposes were wholly alien to me and all warm-blooded creatures like me, so alien that I could not imagine their true forms and missions. What service had this road and the others like it rendered them? Why had it come to be?

The first few steps convinced me that it had never been intended for human feet to follow. For it possessed a rounded raised center which made us slip and slide. In order to maintain our footing we were forced to slacken our pace to a mere crawling shuffle.

I can not tell for how many miles and how many hours we followed that straight, unbranching path. But thrice we stopped to nap and break out meals from the supplies we carried. There was nothing to see or hear, only the darkness, pierced for a few feet by the power of our lenses.

During the third stop Thran brought out his fish-skin map and Analia trained the light from her belt upon it so that he might trace out the way we had come and the way we had yet to go.

"There is a sharp turn to the right and that is the path we must take. We must be almost upon it now."

"Then let us go on to it," said Zacat, rising to his feet. "So far there has been little in this snake hole to interest a fighting man. Where dwells the danger from which Kem-mec fled to fill his master's ear with wild tales?"

"Before us somewhere, my Lord. And I have some belief in Kem-mec and his tales. Shall we go on and prove them?" He rolled up the map and put it back in his pouch.

We rose to our tired feet and went on. As Thran had shown us on the map, our road split abruptly into two, one spur going to the right. Anatan and his sister had already turned into it when a gleam on the surface of the other branch caught my eye. My fingers closed upon a second small shred of robe. I held out my find to the others.

"Could the map be wrong?" I demanded of Thran. "This says so."

"Unless that is bait on a false trail."

"True. But there is only one way to make sure."

"And that?"

"Divide our party. Each follow a spur. See, I shall set a small infrared charge in my ray rod. For as long as it burns I will follow this road. If I come upon nothing during that time to uphold my choice I shall return here and follow yours. You do the same."

Thran agreed at once. "That is the wisest course. Who goes with you?"

"Zacat," answered that individual at once. "We have hunted together before."

"It is well." He hunted through his pouch to find and adjust the charge in the rod at his belt and I did the same. When at last the two were burning we bade each other farewell for a time, setting out upon the routes we had chosen, Thran, Anatan, and Analia to the right, Zacat and I straight ahead. My hand closed about those two scraps in my pouch as we went.

We had gone some distance when Zacat lifted the edge of his mask and sniffed the air.

"Do you scent nothing?"

I followed his example. The musty dryness of the air was tinged with a faint odor, an odor at once sweet and yet faintly corrupting.

"Aye," I answered.

"I like it not. There is a stink like that in some of

those old mountain tombs. Something unpleasant awaits us ahead. But that is little reason for holding back."

The stench grew worse as we advanced and to my amazement the light from my ray rod slowly changed color, taking on a purplish hue. I called this to Zacat's attention.

"Some devilish business. There are things better for men to leave alone. Our friend of Koom has been hunting in forbidden ways. But now he is being hunted, which is a different matter. Let us rout out this smell."

We abruptly came to a sharp turn in the path, the first we had encountered. Cautiously rounding the bend, we found ourselves on the edge of nowhere. . . .

7

The Thing from the Gulf

The path ended abruptly on the lip of an immeasurable gulf. From its depth came a faint sighing murmur, a distant hum as if some form of life crawled and had its being far beneath us.

"The end," said Zacat. "Our choice was the wrong one."

"I wonder," I mused. Something suspended out in the gulf had caught my eye. Two long chains, of the same substance as that which walled the Ways, hung taut and steady as if they supported some unseen weight. I unhooked my ray rod and held it before me so that the pencil of light from the still burning charge could pick out what might hang between the chains.

"Ah—" Zacat purred like a giant Ana, for the ray revealed a bridge of some light-resisting substance, a bridge that ran on out into the curtain of darkness.

Moving the ray I traced the outlines of the bridge to see where it touched on our side of the gulf. It did not touch. A good three feet away it ended in a mass of broken splinters. Whether the break was new or centuries old we had no way of telling, but it might prove an effective barrier.

I measured the length of the tunnel behind us. A man, if he were dexterous and had a good head for heights, might cross the gap with a running leap—if On were good to him. But, let the bridge be with smooth surface, let it display the curved ridge which had proved a hindrance to us from the first, and the gulf yawned below.

Zacat was as quick as I to see our only chance.

"One must stay here," he said, "and hold his ray upon the end of that death trap while the other tries for it. Then, if by the Favor of On he makes it, he must hold his torch in position until the other joins him. Simple but deadly." He laughed.

His solution was the only one. Tightening my belt and lashing my provision bag firmly to my shoulders, I made ready. Then, before he could protest, I thrust my ray rod into his hand and turned back down the corridor. With a leaping run I passed Zacat, who was crouched to one side with rod firm, to light up my landing place.

Then I was out over the depths, my heart pounding with a sickening beat in my ears. My feet touched the glassy surface of the bridge—and slipped. With a scrambling lunge, I threw myself forward, my straining fingers closing upon that middle ridge. And the curve, which had seemed our greatest hazard, saved me. I clutched it grimly, lying facedown on that faint shadowy surface until my wildly pumping heart quieted. Then, with the aid of one of the giant supporting chains, I was able to regain my feet.

From my provision pouch I drew two coils of the thin tough hide rope with which Thran had thoughtfully provided us. With one I lashed myself to the chain, the other I weighted with a tin of the supplies and tossed it across the void to Zacat. He tied my ray rod to it and I pulled it back.

While it was swinging through space to me I endured perhaps the weirdest experience that any man upon my world had ever imagined. For when the ray no longer beat upon the bridge it disappeared from sight and I seemed to be standing on thin air out over empty space, although I could feel the hard pavement beneath my feet.

In a moment the torch was in my hand. Again the splintered end of the bridge appeared out of nothingness.

Zacat made his preparations and disappeared back along the way we had come. Then he came hurtling out of the mouth of the corridor toward me. Perhaps he had exerted some force I had lacked for he landed well in and I was able to draw him to his feet in safety.

"A demon's nest if there ever existed one," he puffed when he again stood upright. "And I do not care to think of a return journey. Nay, let us light both torches. I, for one, have no desire to tread upon empty air, even if my feet say otherwise."

I unfastened myself from my chain anchorage and we set out on that incredible journey over the abyss. Master builders and engineers the Older Ones must have been, but how alien their minds to those of the human race. I marveled at the courage of that Kemmec who penetrated these Ways alone, protected only by the feeble equipment of his time. Perhaps that break in the bridge explained why he had not returned from his last venture.

"That stench is growing stronger," Zacat broke in upon my thoughts.

He raised his torch and flashed it on far ahead. Just

within the circle of light something moved. Zacat stopped short.

"This is indeed a well-cursed place. Something awaits us there, it seems. I never thought I would come to believe in night demons. Yet that thing, or shadow, appeared in my light. Do you realize what that means?"

I did only too well. That something was invisible in ordinary light, as invisible as the bridge when not under infrared rays. And it was coming toward us.

"I say remain here," Zacat continued when he saw that I had caught the significance of his words. "It is better to allow the unknown to reveal its strength first so that you can smell out its weakness. And speaking of smells—"

The odor of corruption and obscene decay was heavy on the dead air and growing stronger with every passing moment. And now it seemed I could catch a faint sound, a sullen scraping.

Again Zacat raised his torch and shot its ray before us. A sizable *something* lumbered backward out of the beam.

"Well, whatever it is, it has no liking for this light," observed my companion with satisfaction. "That is a weakness we can take advantage of. Charge your other rod and we will force it back."

With four rods beaming we strode forward. And always that which disputed our passage gave way before us. We never saw more of it than a dark bulk moving clumsily but swiftly out of the edge of our rays.

The end came soon enough. That which fled from us regained its courage, or perhaps solved the secret of our lights, for the next time we advanced it did not move, but squatted there, awaiting us.

I have seen the nightmare reptiles of the under-

ground Lapidian swamps and the flying horrors of
the Holian salt plains, but what faced us on the invisible bridge in the Ways was far more loathsome to
human sight than those. In the first place it was all
but impossible to see, existing only as a faint cloudy
outline except in the light of our rods. It possessed no
concrete shape, for its body structure seemed oddly
fluid as if it could change its appearance at will.

But the most terrifying thing about it were the eyes
which burned like dull purple lamps in the rolls of its
pudgy gray flesh. It seemed to have no limbs, only
massive chunks of fat tipped with suction pads with
which it drew its fiend-conceived body along.

"By the foul night birds of Dept," swore Zacat,
"there crawls that which would make a man disbe-
lieve his own eyes. If such was what Kem-mec
feared—"

Exhibiting none of the speed with which it had
previously eluded us, it began to crawl forward, its
pads making that thin scraping sound which I had
noted. But the eyes held us fast in a web of horrified
fascination.

The thing before us had a thinking brain. Far
removed from ours perhaps, but one which was even
greater in the powers it possessed. There was intelligence of a high order lighting those strange eyes.

As yet the crawler was as puzzled by us as we
were by it. I could feel the wave of curiosity which
exuded. It was not, I felt, evil as we know evil. For
as I faced those burning eyes I was granted a glimpse
of a terrifyingly alien race and its incredible civilization. A race far removed from our own standards of
morality. So, though I felt nausea and a certain horror, I did not feel fear.

While it was still some distance from us it drew
itself together and reared up, giving the impression of

one pausing to sit and think out a bewildering problem. Briefly it eyed us and then, turning its round, worm-like head, looked down into the gulf.

From far below came a thin wailing cry. Then up out of the darkness whirled a streak of shining silver, soaring on wide pinions. Gracefully it wheeled and fluttered about the bridge and at last closed its wings and came to stand beside the formless monstrosity.

It was human in form; that is, it possessed a shapely body and limbs which corresponded to our arms and legs. But all four limbs ended in suction pads like those of the crawler. Its head was round and seemed to have no features except large purple eyes. A fringed membrane served it for hair. This latter slowly waved erect as it faced us, until the skin stood out about the round head like a nebula of light.

A message beat in upon my brain.

"Why do you tread the ancient Ways, human?"

I knew something of thought transference as practiced by the Learned Ones so now I carefully thought out my answer instead of speaking it aloud.

"I trail an enemy of my own world."

The silver one turned to the crawler and I received an impression of some question asked and answered between them. Then again came inquiry.

"He has passed this way?"

"So I believe."

My answer seemed to arouse the creatures. I knew somehow that they were disturbed, shaken out of their usual serenity. But now I had a question of my own to ask.

"You are of those we call the Older Ones?"

I could feel their amused disdain. "Nay, we are but the clay they shaped upon their potter's wheels. The Older Ones have long since gone. We remain. There is something we must do. Fool, fool! To waste your days hunting down enemies when doom is falling fast upon this puny world!''

"What do you mean?''

"Ask the one who has passed through the forbidden Ways before you. Seek him, human.''

Then all communication between us ceased, for suddenly opalescent lights played along the bulk of the crawler. It reared and plunged. Through its fatty folds appeared great gashes. Its flesh sloughed away in pieces. I trembled under the impact of thought waves beating out untold agony. Its companion rose and hovered above it for an instant, then turned and darted away.

Again the crawler reared and, seemingly blinded, wallowed toward the edge of the bridge. For a moment it tottered there and then plunged over and was gone. We stood alone.

Zacat shook himself as one who would throw off an evil dream.

"What was that all about?'' he demanded.

"The creeping thing met death as these underworlders know it, but not a natural one,'' I replied. "The other probably went to search out the cause.''

"Let us leave this place.'' Zacat shuddered as he looked down into the void which had swallowed up the dying crawler.

We set out again on that slippery track and now we put aside caution, for we wanted to feel the firmness of solid ground under us again. The choke in my throat and sharp pangs in my middle urged me to seek nourishment but Zacat would not pause, saying that it would be best to reach the end of the bridge before we halted again. We saw no more of the winged figure nor did we come upon another crawler and I might almost have to come to believe that we had been the prey of our own imaginations had it not been for later happenings.

In time we came to the end of that eerie bridge and this time stepped with ease from invisibility to solid surface. But Zacat stumbled, pitching forward to his knees. When he scrambled up again, he held a slender metal cone, the distributor of a destructive ray.

"I think but for the crawler we would have felt the breath of this." He fingered it reflectively. "That death was meant for us. The Master of Koom has ceased to regard us as amusing."

There was a whir and flutter in the air above our heads. Supported on wide-stretched wings hung the silver shape from the gulf. It lingered there for a second and then was gone again, but in that moment I had endured the chill of a cold and deadly hatred, directed not toward me but against the one who had dropped that telltale cone.

Zacat looked at me with no small satisfaction. "It seems that two hunters have become three. And that thing from the gulf is not a pleasant enemy. Kepta has stirred up the depths of Hell itself now. But may On grant that we reach him first!"

Heartily echoing that wish I stepped into the curved track. Having confirmed, by the death of the crawler, that we were on the right path, I felt at liberty to snap off the rays from our rods, so conserving that portion of the charge yet remaining.

Our journey for long hours was merely a repetition of that we had made on the other side of the broken bridge. The trail ran straight on between blank walls. There was naught to see or hear. Three times we rested and ate, then went on again. I wondered if Thran, true to our bargain, was following us and what he would make of the way across the gulf.

I had lost all track of time in that sunless, lightless

burrow, but it must have been several days after last meeting the silver thing that we came abruptly into a region where the walls gave off a soft phosphorescent glow. This increased as we advanced until at last we were able to discard our masks altogether.

The corridor we were following ended at the foot of a ramp and without hesitation we began the ascent. At the top a heavy door of some substance foreign to that which lined the Way stood closed.

We threw our weight against it and, after a space of straining effort upon our part, it began to give. Having edged it open until the crack was large enough for us to squeeze through, we drew our rods and entered.

The doorless corridor in which we stood was wholly modern and of our own world; the alien atmosphere of the Ways was gone. Stealthily we slipped along, our scale-clad feet making, in spite of all our efforts, faint whispering sounds on the floor.

At the end of the corridor we were confronted by another door. Here again we were forced to exert our full strength to move its massive bulk.

I could not still the cry of utter amazement which came to my lips as we huddled inside that second door. A gigantic laboratory lay before us. My untrained mind could not grasp the meaning of one thousandth of the monstrous appliances which were gathered there. We stood in the secret workroom of Kepta where even the Learned Ones had never penetrated.

Zacat, refusing to be impressed by what he did not understand, advanced along a lower runway in this collection of super-scientific apparatus. But a moment later his confidence oozed from him with a single stifled exclamation. And when I joined him I saw a row of crystal-lidded boxes lining that narrow passage. Even now I will not allow myself to dwell on what those boxes contained. It will suffice to say that the brain responsible for the contents must have been utterly, inhumanly mad.

With eyes averted from that gruesome sight, we ran down the passage, our caution gone from us. If I had not hated Kepta before to the innermost core of me, I would have loathed him after that single glimpse of the results of his beastly experiments.

Again we came to a ramp winding upward. Eager to be gone from that place of mad horrors, we ascended. The hall at its head was a short one, a mere anteroom for some chamber behind a masking curtain. The murmur of voices stopped me as I reached to brush aside the fabric.

"Thus it lies, my dear Thrala. Is it not clear?" Kepta's suave voice came through to us.

But the answer was muffled as if the speaker gazed upon some terrifying sight.

"It is clear."

"Then you will agree with me that our hope lies—"

The words slurred into an indistinguishable mumble as if Kepta had moved away from us. I waited no longer. Reaching out, I tore away the curtain.

8

World Doom

"Garan!" Thrala's eyes, wide with astonishment, held mine.

Kepta whirled, a snarl distorting his lips. "Sept! I thought you—"

"Dead, Kepta? Not yet—your ray killed another."

"Thran!" Again Thrala cried out.

"No. A thing out of the gulf. Its companion has smelled out your guilt. I would keep far from the Ways, Kepta. That is, if you live to cross the threshold of this chamber. What shall it be for us? Steel against steel, or naked strength? This is the reckoning."

He laughed in my face, his momentary disturbance gone.

"Do you think I would stoop to exchange blows with such as you, soldier? Here I am master, as you shall speedily learn."

He stepped back toward the far wall. I did not need Thrala's cry to warn me. I leaped, but I was too late. Under his hand the wall seemed to melt and he was gone. I struck a solid surface to be thrown back, bruised, to the pavement.

"He's as slippery as a saurian of the depths," observed Zacat with heat.

Thoroughly enraged at my own clumsiness I would have tried to beat in that wall had not the uselessness of such an endeavor been apparent from the first. Instead I set upon a search for some door which would let me through to track down the Master of Koom.

"No!" Thrala pulled me back. "There remains no time for private feuds or vengeance. Look!"

She pointed down at a plate set in the pavement. On a dull black surface glimmered and glowed tiny pin pricks of light.

"What is it?" I asked stupidly.

"Krand's doom has come upon her and all of us!" Never have I heard such a tone of stark finality as that which ravaged Thrala's voice.

"Do you not understand? This is a map of the heavens, the stars, the myriad worlds that share with us this universe. And now one of those far distant worlds has been thrown out of its accustomed path, hurled into space, a missile aimed by the gods at Krand! For untold centuries it has been traveling toward us and there was a time when we might have escaped—" She hesitated and her finger plucked at her torn gown.

"Might have escaped, do you understand? Stood free and watched destruction pass us by! But Kepta lost us that chance, our one chance. He needed power for his loathsome experiments so he committed the unpardonable act, the deed which the Learned Ones pledged themselves a hundred thousand years ago never to attempt. He harnessed the power of our sun!

"And because the rhythm of our solar system was

so delicately balanced, he ruined us. Inch by inch through the past years our orbit has changed. We Learned Ones knew, knew it from the first, but we could not find the cause. And now that cause lies plain before us—too late!''

"But Kepta—when he knew it meant destruction—''

She laughed wildly, stamping upon those pin pricks which were stars. "Kepta is wise, he is cunning. Never will he be caught in his own trap. He plans to leave Krand behind, to search out a new world to conquer with the aid of his dark knowledge, somewhere beyond the stars. But Krand shall be left to face the fate he dragged down upon her!''

"But the Learned Ones, surely—'' I began again.

She stared at me for a moment and then the wildness seemed to fade from her face, leaving her once again the calm, nerveless woman who had dared to play Ila within the pleasure palace of Sotan.

"You are right to rebuke me, Garan. We have no time for wild words and purposeless actions now. Let us get back to Yu-Lac and see what can be done there. And at once, lest Kepta arrive with his guards as he has threatened.''

"Back through the Ways then,'' I decided. "All Koom must be aroused against us now. But the bridge—''

"That can be crossed when we arrive,'' said Zacat. "Listen!''

From somewhere within those walls a sullen murmur swelled. Thrala clutched at me. "They are coming! Kepta—''

"And we—go! Come.''

Back we traced our way through that awe-inspiring laboratory, down that passage lined with bottled monsters, out through the two ponderous doors into the dark of the Ways. And here Thrala had to cling fast to me, for, not being equipped with our darkness-piercing lenses, she moved blindly. But I did not find the situation unwelcome.

Although we stumbled quickly along that ridged way the sound of pursuit rang ever in our ears, echoing loudly through the vaults of the Ways. At last Thrala paused, stretching out a hand against the wall to steady herself.

"You go on"—her breath hissed between her teeth—"go on to Yu-Lac, I am done."

I laughed and yet saw the kernel of wisdom in her words.

"You speak true, one of us must remain to keep this pack in check. Zacat, take the princess and go!"

"Do you not see, Garan? It is I who cannot hold the pace. Give me your ray rod—"

Then in truth I saw that she was done; she could not match her failing strength to ours. There was only one answer. I turned to Zacat.

"Go!"

He shook his head with sullen finality, forcing me to evoke my last weapon.

"It is an order," I said sharply.

His head went up and he looked me eye to eye. "As you command, so must I obey. You have left me nothing—not even pride."

And so he turned and went from us, moving slowly at first, as if the weight of years had fallen suddenly upon him. Thrala looked up at me.

"Go, go! Do not leave this, too, upon my heart."

I smiled. "Three years ago I foresaw this, but dimly, perhaps. It is my fate to serve you, Lady, and so will it be until the end. You, out of your graciousness, gave me something to strive for. And On is good. For I will prove myself in your eyes at the end."

"Garan!" She faced me clear-eyed. "Garan, since this is the end for us, Krand and its foolish customs no longer mattering—Garan, do you not understand? I am yours for the taking, as I have been for three long years, years of minutes, hours, and days, with thoughts of you stringing them all together like a golden cord. What need have we of scented lovemaking, of sweet dalliance? We know!"

And then her arms were about me and I felt her lips press mine with fierce intensity. The Ways, Kepta, Krand—all were forgotten as we stood in the rose-misted heart of our dream. Thrala was mine! Mine! Her soft flesh quivered beneath my hands, her hair, that glorious hair I had so many times thought of, brushed my cheek.

So few were the moments we stole from time, so scanty our loving, yet it enriched my life forever and I knew, be my days many or few, I would walk proudly through them because of these moments.

"Must it end thus?" she whispered.

And now, at her question, the will to live swelled within me and I no longer calmly accepted the fate before us. "If we make the bridge—" I caught her up, and started on.

The eerie surroundings must have frightened our pursuers into a hesitating advance for the sound behind grew muffled as we went on. Now, filled with the will to win free, to savor this amazing gift of Thrala's beneath the open heavens, I kept on, my strength seeming to grow with the passing moments. We were forced to rest at intervals and when Thrala had recovered she went, surefooted, before me, holding one of the ray rods to make our path plain. At our last stop before we reached the bridge I forced her to give in to my wishes and don my protecting scale suit, leaving me only the detachable mask. The air of the Ways felt cold and damp against my skin, for, save for a waist cloth, I was bare. But Thrala was safe.

Again we ventured out upon that unseen span which the engineers of that lost race had thrown across the gulf. As we advanced slowly, foot by foot, along the shadowy surface our torch revealed, the sound of the chase behind us swelled once more into clamor. And, when we were perhaps a third of the way across, the lights they carried were to be seen clustered about the head.

At that distance we could make out only black figures moving back and forth, but it was plain to see that Kepta's men had no stomach for following us out upon the invisibility which confronted them. So, after much loud argument, only a single shape detached itself from the cluster and moved cautiously in our wake.

"Kepta!" cried Thrala softly.

I wondered what arms he carried and, sick with fear, pushed Thrala on ahead lest he try some devilishness with a destruction ray. To my surprise he did not, he only came after us with grim determination. And when he was a good way out upon the bridge startled cries of fear and horror came from his men. They scattered in flight, pelting back the way they had come and left the gulf to the three of us.

Kepta, after one long look at his retreating followers, came steadily on and I knew then that he was hot for our deaths. I put Thrala aside, for it was in my mind to go to meet him. When I saw the yellow flames which flickered in his eyes, I understood that his black, destroying hatred of me had vanquished his caution. To satisfy that rage burning within him he must break me with his own two hands. He had put aside his weapons.

So we edged toward one another, balancing carefully on that thread of safety. Thrala held her torch so that I could see my footing but Kepta had no such aid, placing his feet by instinct only. As I went, I put aside my mask and provision bag and stood free. He, too, was stripped for battle, but, as I crept up within striking distance, his hand dropped to his wide belt and for a fraction of a second I caught a glimpse of steel.

Then, like fighting jungle reptiles, we came together. The slaver from his grinning jaws dripped upon my flesh. My fingers vised around the wrist of that sinisterly closed fist and my other hand groped for his throat. He was a clever and knowledgeable fighter, Kepta of Koom. I have held my own in a hundred barrack fights, but never had I been matched with such a bundle of rippling muscle and fighting nerve.

I tried all the tricks I knew one after another only to discover that he held the perfect counter to each. The running sweat made our flesh clammy, slippery under grasping fingers, our sight blurred. Once he twisted almost free and I felt a searing pain lash across my lower ribs, but the blow did not fall true and, before he could strike again, I closed in upon him. Then it was that I saw a shade pass over that hate-ravaged face so close to mine, the flush of anger faded from his cheeks and I guessed that wisdom had returned to him, forcing him to realize that he should never have met me upon a ground of my own choosing. No longer did he strive to bring me down, now his fight was all for freedom, freedom wherein to use some weapon other than his own strength.

Like the slimy saurian Zacat had compared him to, he twisted and writhed while I strove merely to keep my slipping holds. Then with a lunge he broke my hold, flinging himself out of my reach with the same movement.

He stumbled, then, picking himself up, went flying back toward the bridge head. It was no use for me to attempt to follow; a dizziness sent me swaying perilously close to the edge of the abyss. My outstretched hand closed upon one of those great chains which held the span and there I clung, sick and weak.

"Garan!"

I raised my head with an effort.

"Back!" I cried and my voice rang hollow. "Take the mask and stand clear. He plans to blast us with the ray."

In answer she strode forward to where I wavered against the supporting chain.

"I think not," she answered steadily. "See, even as you foretold, vengeance rises out of the gulf!"

Through the mists which still clouded my vision I saw the silver shapes which came spiraling up out of the maw of the dark. With a steady beating of their mighty wings they passed us and were gone, like war arrows, on the trail of Kepta.

What happened when they dropped upon the flying Koomian, what dreadful business was wrought there in the dark, we could not see. But when there came a shuddering cry, a shout of mingled fear and unearthly dread, I guessed that those of this inner world had repaid their debt in full. The fruits of Kepta's unhallowed seeking had at last brought about his end.

Back through the murk came the bird shapes, sweeping by without a glance at us. And did or did not one of them bear a limp figure between his sucker pads? I thought he did, but perhaps my eyes betrayed me.

We thought that they were gone when one last one came over us. He circled and shot downward until his sucker feet just touched the surface of the bridge.

For the third time those weird purple eyes in that featureless face dwelt upon me.

"So, human, having gained your desire, you return to the outer world? But I think you shall not have long there. We, too, may read the warning set among the stars we have never seen. Krand has brought us forth, now we may leave her like an outgrown skin. Pass free from fear of us, human, we stand eons apart."

The fanning of his wings grew swifter, he arose and was gone with lazy sweeps into the gulf. We were alone.

But even as we lingered there, trying to gather our wits, a distant shouting from before us rumbled in our ears.

"There is help," I said. It seemed to me that Thrala shivered and a change came across her face as if some mask were slipping back into place. She turned slowly with all the lightness gone out of her steps.

Together we went forward and now and then I raised my voice in answer to those questing shouts. Before long we caught sight of the glow from their ray rods.

But instead of quickening her pace Thrala went yet more slowly and her eyes were ever upon me, but I could not read the meaning of the shadow in their depths. She drooped as if some chill wind had torn her. A rich exultation filled me. Had she not lain willingly in my arms? Was she not mine?

Zacat, Anatan, and Thran were crouched there beyond the broken end of the bridge. They had rigged a network of ropes so that we might swing across to them in comparative safety, escaping the uncertainty of my first leap. Thrala went first and when I saw her land safely in Thran's grasp I made the ropes fast about my own body. A moment's swing across the darkness and Anatan's hands were upon me, pulling me in.

"Kepta?" the Gorlian demanded.

"Those of the gulf have claimed him."

"You are hurt!" Anatan's hand had slid across the congealed blood on my ribs.

"A scratch only."

But by the light of Analia's radium cell Thran examined it, binding up the slight wound with a strip of silk from his pouch. Then he produced the extra scale suit he had carried and aided me to don it. All this time my eyes were ever upon Thrala, where she stood apart with her handmaiden. And to my growing uneasiness I saw that she was avoiding meeting my gaze.

"So Kepta is gone," observed Thran as I fumbled with the fastening of my sword belt.

"Aye, the manner of his going was not a pleasant one." I went on to describe the coming and going of the winged shapes from the gulf.

"Kepta gone," the Gorlian mused. "Koom's hold broken at last. There remains—Krand."

I saw Thrala's head go up. "Aye"—her voice was steady though her lips trembled—"there remains Krand."

9

Escape

Hastily we retraced our way, for, now that we knew the sum of what lay before us, we were eager to reach the surface. I did not doubt that there was some mode of escape from the coming disaster. Those shapes from the gulf had hinted of such and Thrala declared that Kepta's preparations for flight were almost complete.

What Kepta had done, we could do, if there remained enough time. So one part of my mind was busy with the thought of escape while yet another portion dwelt upon those moments in the Ways when Thrala and I had snatched joy from the mouth of death. And thinking of her as she was then, I could not understand her constant avoidance of me now. She hurried ahead, keeping Analia ever by her side, while I was forced to answer the questions Thran rained upon me.

His quest down the side branch of the Ways had led him into a strange, deadly swamp-like hollow where weird and awful forms of life lurked amid gigantic fungi. At one time he and his companions had been forced to blast their path clear with their ray rods. But when they had discovered no other clues during the time set, they had returned to take our road and had so arrived at the bridge just in time to see Zacat leap the gap.

Once more we came to the ramp leading up out of this place of alien horrors and moved through the hall where the dancers of Qur had woven their strange patterns. Around us the pleasure palace lay silent and deserted. There were traces of its inhabitants' hurried flitting in every chamber through which we passed. But nowhere did we see anyone.

Again Analia piloted us through the passages in its walls but this time we took one which led us under the city street level to open in the end upon the fringe of the royal gardens, a passage which had been constructed by Thrala's orders when their mad venture in the pleasure palace had first been planned.

It was night when we stepped out into the fresh coolness of the dew-wet sod. And I was glad to again breathe deep the rain-washed air of the upper world. We had no way of determining how long we had been in the Ways.

Quickly we struck across the gardens, for it was Thran's plan that we show ourselves directly to the Emperor and tell our story. When we reached the bulk of the palace, he avoided the more public halls and walks, following a roundabout route to an inner chamber.

He gave a single peremptory rap upon the door and then pushed it open. We had burst in thus unceremoniously upon a full meeting of the council. And at the sight of Thrala the Emperor arose to his feet with a cry. Then they were all crowding about us, demanding instant answers to their myriad questions.

I listened to Thran's jerky recital of our tale, but I was watching Thrala and had little attention for him or his listeners. When the Gorlian had come to an end the Emperor drew a deep breath.

"So, that was the way of it. It is well for Kepta that he does not stand before us now. But a vengeance worse than any we could have conceived has been wreaked if you speak true. Koom is no longer a meance. There remains this doom the Master has brought upon us. Let not one word of this matter escape your lips, Krand must not be sent mad. Our life, upon the surface, must be as usual, but in secret we can prepare for the end. How long do we have, daughter?" He turned to Thrala.

"Kepta said three months before the worst of the disturbances begin."

"So short a time? Then we must bend our backs to mighty labors. Give us ten hours' time to assemble our forces and then we will meet here again."

Thus abruptly he dismissed us. Thrala and Analia slipped through the far door without a backward look. Zacat, Anatan, and I left as inconspicuously as possible for my headquarters. Thran remained with the Emperor.

Having gained the shelter of my own apartments, I bathed and then flung myself upon my sleeping couch, there to toss open-eyed, my brain awhirl with all the problems which confronted me. At length I drowsed, falling into dream-filled slumber.

At that second extraordinary meeting of the council we met those of the Learned Ones whom the Emperor relied upon and certain members of the other castes considered trustworthy. And there for a good four hours or more the leading astronomer of Krand lectured us concerning our destroyer and our companion worlds.

It had been proven in the past that life as we knew it could not exist on either of the two other planets which shared our sun. But other solar systems lay open to us. One such, lying some hundreds of light-years away, boasted nine planets, one of which was newly-born. That raw new world was to be our goal.

When this had been provisionally decided upon they turned to me for advice about spaceships. I laid before them what little I knew.

"The acceleration needed to break the grip of Krand's gravity upon a spaceship would kill the voyagers before it had torn through our layers of atmosphere. It must be a ship radically different in design from any we have ever conceived and one with more power than any now existing."

Thran nodded. "But we can furnish power in abundance now," he said grimly.

"You mean?"

"Kepta's source lies open to our use. Solar power."

The others drew a little away from him. "Would you break the ancient oath again?" asked the Emperor quietly.

Thran looked around at us. "We must face plainly what lies before us. For Krand and most of her people there is no future. For a handful, a handful who will carry on our race and build anew better than we have done—for them there is hope. A single ship such as Lord Garan has spoken of, a ship endowed with inexhaustible solar power may win free. The question which lies before us now is will we throw ourselves and our world into a period of agonizing labor that a minute portion of our number may win across the void to safety. Dare we say that we are worthy of such sacrifice upon the part of our fellows?"

The Emperor turned toward a white-robed figure on his right, the High Priest of the Temple of Knowledge. He smoothed his robe with his wrinkled palms and his old, old eyes seemed to stare into the future.

"On has disclosed to us this way; are we too fearful to walk in a path He has pointed out to us?" he asked slowly. "If those who go are worthy, then we have accomplished the task set before us. But this I say, men of Krand, the day of the Learned Ones is past. It was our sin that has brought this upon our world and therefore there must be, during these last few days still left to us, no Learned Ones and commoners, only brothers striving shoulder to shoulder for the common good."

A faint murmur followed his speech and my heart stirred. Barrier so banished, then Thrala was surely mine, come what may. I was free to claim publicly what she had given when death was upon us in the Ways.

"Lord Garan"—with an effort I recalled my wandering thoughts and looked to the Emperor—"more than any of us you know the secrets of air construction. Our experts are under your command. What have you to offer us?"

"There is a man, a certain Hay-leen of Campt, who has been experimenting in interplanetary ships for the past two years. He has been successful in landing a rocket upon our neighbor, Soyu. But it will be necessary to take him wholly into our confidence."

"Do you trust him?"

I hesitated. "I know very little of Hay-leen except as I have made contact with him during his work. He has reported to me the progress of his experiments once each month during the past year. But I know nothing of him personally. However, he is the only man on Krand today who has the ability to solve our problem."

"Hm." The Emperor caressed the line of his jaw

with his fingers. "Lord Zacat, what of your Ruian mines? Can you increase their output, double it perhaps during the next month?"

"Give me a free hand and I will try," said the officer with grim caution, but his reply seemed to please the Emperor.

"Then it remains to select some waste place, proper for laying the keel of our ship, and there setting to work. At a time I shall appoint, Lord Garan, relieve your engineer of duty and order him to report to me. Lord Zacat will receive new shipping orders for Ru. And, please On, we shall keep our council until the last. Are we agreed, my Lords?"

One by one they gave their assent and so it was decided.

The next month was a period of nightmare, undersurface activity for us all. At the same time the unrest Kepta had so skillfully sowed flourished and grew, so that there were constant threats of rebellion and riot to make my office no easy one. Had it not been for Anatan, whom I came to rely upon more and more with each day of trouble, I could never have kept my corps in order.

The young Holian seemed to have aged years and stood ready at my call at any hour. Next to my desire for his help and my liking for him I had another motive in keeping him by me, for only through him did I hear of Thrala. Analia, his sister, continued as Thrala's first lady-in-waiting and she was in constant attendance upon the Princess. And in all that time I had not met Thrala face to face.

I was sitting alone one evening in my chamber, studying the reports from Ru containing Zacat's personal comments upon the situation there, when Anatan entered. He dropped a small metal message case on the table before me. The roll of silk within bore but a single line:

"The grotto at moonrise."

There was no signature and I smoothed it out perplexedly.

"Where did you get this?"

"From Analia," he answered shortly.

Knowing then from whose hand it must have come, I thrust it hurriedly into my belt pouch. But Anatan lingered by my side, irresolution written plain upon his face.

"Well?"

He spread out his hands in a helpless gesture. "It is unfair!" The cry seemed torn from his lips and then he turned and ran from me as if I had been a demon of the night.

Wondering greatly at the cause of his outbreak, I wandered to my windows. It was not far from moonrise and, my heart pounding wildly within me, I caught up a long dark cloak which would adequately conceal my uniform. With this about me I hurried out.

My private flier touched the palace landing stage and I hurried down the ramp, murmuring the password to the sentries as I went. The garden winds were cool and never had doomed Krand seemed so fair in my eyes as on that night when I passed through the Emperor's glades in search of that grotto where we had lingered once before.

I was early. There was no one awaiting me among the trees. Burning with impatience, I paced back and forth across the shadow-filled dell. But I did not have long to wait. Through the dusk came a white figure I knew well.

"Thrala!"

My arms closed about her yielding body, my lips

caught the freshness of her flesh. But she struggled free and, with her hands to her mouth, shrank from me.

"What have I done, beloved? Frightened you?"

She shook her head and then in a bar of moonshine I saw the silent tears slipping down her white cheeks.

"It is I who am at fault, Garan—"

"You are tired, perhaps?" I broke in eagerly. "Indeed, I would not trouble you, sweet."

"No, no!" Her voice arose to a sharp cry. "How can I say it!"

Her thin fingers twisted together and still the tears dropped to wet the bosom of her robe. Then she seemed to gain some measure of self-control.

"You have done nothing—nothing, Garan, that was not right and beautiful and good always. You and I will have that to remember when—when—" Her voice failed.

And now I was trembling and a chill struck at my very bones for I knew somehow that happiness was denied to me.

"What is it that you have to say to me, Thrala?" I asked as gently as I might. "Do not be afraid of me, beloved."

"I am not free to live and love, Garan. Not free to choose joy in life. The decree has gone forth, for the good of Krand I am Thran's. And know now the depths of my sin. For I was Thran's when I stood in the Ways and called out the love you bore me. I have been Thran's since my return from the Temple of Light. Turn from me now, Garan, as you have the right. I have betrayed our love, being weak."

Now I felt the chill which had come upon me creep into my heart. "You are Thran's mate?" I asked between stiffened lips.

She raised her head high. "No, nor did I ever think I would be. When I first faced you in the control cabin of my father's ship, when our eyes met and looked deep into each other's secret heart, then I knew that no other might I ever honestly take to mate. For you are mine, Garan, and I am yours, though worlds swing between us. So have we been before and so shall we be again! When they urged Thran upon me I delayed and set aside, dallying ever, hoping that fate might some day prove kind. And when we stood close in the Ways, I thought that death had come to solve our desperate riddle, so I spoke. But we won through and now the end has come to all my scheming. This day Thran was chosen to lead the flight from Krand and I go with him. My duty has been made cruelly plain. I must set aside love. Aside, Garan—"

Her voice grew weak and at length faded away. She sank down upon the bench, staring wide-eyed out through the trees which masked our retreat. I laughed harshly and the bitterness of that sound was sharp even in my own ears.

"So the soldier must stand aside. You have decided that, you Learned Ones. Well, what if the soldier will not, Thrala? What if I claim what you tell me is rightfully mine?"

"Garan." There was a new force within her. "Garan, cruelly have I wrought, but do not force me always to remember this hour with more than sorrow. I have tarnished our love, but you would break it."

"I am sorry. I rebel no longer, Royal Lady. Garan shall go back to his place that Krand may profit." And with those words I turned and left her, not heeding the cry which followed me. For red rage gripped me and I saw all the world about me through a crimson mist.

When I stood once more within my own locked chamber I stared at the walls with dull, unseeing eyes. All night I paced the floor. But when morning came I had conquered my inner tumult. Through those bitter hours something within me, perhaps the ghost of my starved and defrauded youth, died forever.

I went through the days which remained to me calmly enough, doing mechanically the tasks which were mine to do. My experts labored in the wilds of Cor where the spaceship slowly took shape in its cradle. Zacat performed wonders in Ru from whence came tales of his ruthless rule. Anatan hovered ever about me, watching with sorrowful eyes. But I went my way alone.

It had been decided to send forth a beam of condensed energy, a directional beam, to strike upon the planet selected for our landing place. Within this gigantic tunnel of pure energy the bullet-like ship would ride secure to its destination. The invisible walls would ward off wandering meteors, safeguarding the voyagers. But there was no time to test our theory. Even now the coming doom hung heavy above us, a glowing ball of orange in the night sky.

Three weeks before the end we were summoned to a last mighty conference in Yu-Lac. It was no longer possible to keep secret the fate of Krand; the end had almost come. There had been eruptions and two tidal waves and a series of earthquakes, growing in intensity.

This night we met to select those who were to venture out into space that some part of our world might be saved. Thran and Thrala sat together and before the Lord of Gorl lay a list of names. It was clear that those adventurers must be young and strong, well able to survive the strain of space travel. And few of those gathered there could so qualify. Yet no shadow lay upon their faces as they listened.

Name after name was read out. I was mightily pleased to hear that both Anatan and Analia were included. But when at length Thran was done, I rose to protest.

"My Lords, withdraw my name."

"But we have need of you—"

I cut through Thran's response. "You will have little need for a solider on your raw new world. I will stay here where I will be of some worth in the disorder of these last days. Nay, I go not. I am Krand's, and Krand's will I be until the end." I looked at Thrala. All the bitterness and hate was gone from me and I faced her smilingly. I saw her hand touch her unsteady lips and then move toward me. I was well content.

So in spite of all their urging I held to the decision I had made. And Anatan would have stayed by me if I had not fairly forced him into the transport flier which was to take them to Cor and the ship. Thrala came to me at the last moment.

"Beloved," she said clearly, "now you have given me a memory which is more precious than the treasure of a thousand kings. Until our next meeting, farewell." And in the sight of all of them she laid her lips to mine.

Then they were gone and we stood on the landing stage looking after that black speck fast fading into the distance. Zacat was the first to stir. He turned to me, his hand outstretched, his old wide grin splitting his plain face.

"You have been a good comrade, Garan. When we meet beyond the stars, we shall have tall tales to tell, you and I. Now, farewell."

"Where are you going?" I demanded.

"Back to Ru. I am soldier enough to wish to remain at my post until the end." And his flier too vanished in the hazy sky.

I was alone.

10

Darkness

We were on the crest of Yu-Lac's tallest watch-tower. My body was pressed against the stone; I could feel the chill of that contact through my cloak. But there was the coldness of death itself within me.

"There it rises!" Was it the Emperor who spoke or had the dull pounding of blood in my brain beat out the words?

Behind the distant mountains there was a splotch of flame, a blooming burst of fire. A shattering roar. . . . The murmur of the frenzied city was eaten up and gone. But from the surface of our stricken world arose a javelin of light, up and up. A spear of protest hurtled against the gods.

One deep shuddering sob broke through my control. The Emperor's arm was about my shoulders.

"There passes the heart of Krand. Was it not worth the price, my son?"

"No!" pounded the hot blood in my veins.

I squarely faced his fine eyes.

"Aye," my lips formed the word my heart did not feel.

Even as I watched, the spear of flame spun out into the void. The heavens were dark and drear again. From below came the cries of a world gone mad with fear and hate.

"To the last, son?"

"To the last." I sealed the pact between us.

We turned and, side by side, descended from the watchtower to the street. There we separated, he to attend to his duties, I to mine.

As a soldier I knew that from now on until the end I must use all my powers and all of the men under my command to preserve order. I well understood that this was to be a thankless task. I realized the enormity of it as I hastened to the barracks through the crowded roistering mobs which packed the streets. No force under Krand's sun could hope to bring order from this chaos—but we must try.

Everywhere the mobs milled in hopeless confusion. Some engaged in senseless acts of violence, open street fighting, and looting and gutting of buildings. With a sense of pride which held even now I sighted the bright uniforms of my own soldiers as they literally fought to do what little they could to keep some small control. Every street corner seemed now to have sprouted an oracle. Some of these prayed; others shouted blame for the coming holocaust against the Learned Ones, inciting their listeners to acts of violence in a world gone mad.

I fought my way through, welcoming the physical action which kept me from thinking too much. It was hard to realize that my lady Thrala was gone, if plans had not gone awry, on her way through the great void between the stars to another world and another life in which I would have no part. I was not one to be resigned to such a loss. Far otherwise—then and there did I swear to On that if he allowed me another existence sometime, somewhere upon another world, as some of our people thought could happen, I would once again find the life essence that was Thrala. And then—nothing—no force of God or man would ever separate us.

Holding to that oath as a storm-racked sailor might cling to a life raft, I reached the barracks. Troops filed—trotted—out to face the chaos beyond. One might so watch an Ana trying to restrain a grippon. For every act of violence they prevented there were a thousand more come to a bloody finish.

The next few days were a nightmare of thankless, ceaseless activity. There was no real night—or day— only duty and a terrible fatigue of both mind and body. All sane life in Krand, it seemed, had come to a halt. The pleasure palaces were filled with those seeking forgetfulness. Half the buildings in the city of Yu-Lac had been looted and gutted. We made no arrests—there was no time—nor prisons. We delivered summary justice at the scene of each crime. Only a few continued to lead a normal life and attend to normal duties: my own men, to my continued pride, the police, and most of the Learned Ones. Had one needed proof of the evil wrought by the madness of Kepta, he need only raise his eyes and look.

I was kept so busy in those last days of disintegrating Krand that I had little time to think of Thrala, or to speculate upon the fate of the spaceship.

On the fourth straight day without sleep and little rest, I knew I must seek some easement or fall in my own path. Also I had an errand at the Palace. Wearily I made my way to the roof where my flier was kept. I exited into a chilly, wind-swept, blood-red dawn. Above me the invading planet hung its threat—a hammer to cover a quarter of the sky. I knew, if our Learned Ones were correct, that now the moment was very close when all Krand would break into fragments.

As I rose above the ravaged city I saw that we now had another remorseless enemy. Huge waves of water battered the lower reaches, demolishing walls which had stood unchanged for generations, dealing death to any who had tarried there overlong.

Acting on a sudden premonition, I pushed at top speed for the Palace. The Emperor and I had made a pact; I was sure he would rather meet his end in the clean On-given air. He and I could do no more for the world of our birth.

I flew against the push of a mighty wind with that same need for carrying out orders as had kept me at my post throughout these fear-crazed days. The flier controls were an enemy I must fight with all my strength. Beneath me buildings shuddered, shook like sapling trees in a vicious storm and there was a deafening roar of sound. My craft was no longer answering any control I could assert. As it spun I caught alternating glimpses of sky and ground. Buildings shattered their debris down upon the small running things once of my own kind. Huge waves rolled back, taking with them a rubble of stone-broken bodies.

Darkness—and with it panic which was like a body blow. All else I had expected but this, carrying with it all man's age-old fear, was far worse than any warning could suggest. That lasted only a moment while something too huge to be eye-measured passed and was gone into space. Suddenly, I knew: Krand had split asunder and had added a new moon—or, was that Krand which had gone hurtling by and this the moon?

My flier was completely beyond control, smashed at and buffeted by the howling, screaming wind. Only the pilot's seat webbing had kept me so far from being beaten to death within. Breath—I could no longer breathe— Now, as blackness descended upon me, I saw—not the chaos of a world such as no man might ever look upon and yet live. I saw—Thrala—Thrala as she was and would ever be for me!

For a long moment there was an awed silence between my Lady Thrala and myself—who was now Garan of the Flame in the cavern world of Tav. Those scenes we had just viewed were too vivid in our memories, too hurtful even yet.

And—who was I? Garan of Yu-Lac that was—how far back in time, could any reckon that now? Or Garan that is—in the here and present, who could put out his hand to the lost one and feel hers lie within it?

Thrala—I caught her up, shaken well out of that daze the past had flung over me. Against me, my arms about her, no separation now—ever.

Forgotten was the room in which we stood—the now blank mirrors of seeing.

Search was ended—an end was a beginning.

One Spell Wizard

In all professions there are not only the awe-inspiring great successes, and the forgotten failures, but also those who seem unable to climb the tallest peaks, yet do not tumble hopelessly into the chasms in between. There were sorcerers in High Hallack of whom nobles were quick to speak with reverence when in company; what they said in private remained private if they were lucky. One could never be quite sure of the substance of shadows, nor even of the pedigree of a web-weaving spider. Such uncertainty can be nerve-racking at times.

Also there were warlocks and wizards near to the other end of the scale who barely eked out livings in tumble-down cottages surrounded by unpleasant bogs, or found themselves reduced to caves where water dripped unendingly, and bats provided a litter they could well do without. Their clients were landsmen who came to get a cure for an ailing cow or a stumbling horse. Cow—horse—when a man of magic should be rightfully dealing with the fate of dales, raking in treasure from lords, living in a keep properly patrolled at night by things which snuffled at the doors to keep all unhappy visitors within their chambers from dusk to dawn—or the reverse, depending upon the habits of the visitor. Scorcerers have a very wide range of guests, willing and unwilling.

Wizards have no age, save in wizardry. And to live in a bat- and water-haunted cave for long sours men. Though to begin with wizards are never of a lightsome temperament. A certain acid view of life accompanies the profession.

And Saystrap considered he had been far too long in a cave. It was far past the time when he should have been raised to at least a minor hill keep with a few grisly servitors, if not to the castle of his dreams. There was certainly no treasure in his cave, but he refused to face the fact that there never would be.

The great difficulty was the length of Saystrap's spells: they were a hindrance to his ambition. They worked very well for as much as twenty-four hours—if he expended top effort in their concoction. He was truly a master of some fine effects with those, but when they did not last he was labeled a dismal failure, which was enough to bring all his frustrations to the boiling point.

At last he was driven to accept his limitations to the point of working out a method whereby a short-lived spell could be put to good account. Only to do this he must have an assistant. But, while a sorcerer of note could pick and choose apprentices, a half-failure such as Saystrap had to take what he might find in a very limited labor market.

Not too far from his cave lived a landsman with two sons. The eldest was a credit to his thrifty upbringing, a model young man who was upright enough to infuriate all his contemporaries in the neighborhood, to whom he was constantly cited as an example. He worked from sunrise to early dusk with a will, never spent silver when copper would do—in all ways an irritating youth.

But his brother was as useless a lad as any father wanted to curse out of house and field. He could be found lying on his back with the mowing hardly begun watching clouds—*clouds*, mind you! Put to any task he either broke the tools by some stupid misuse, or ruined what he was supposed to be working on. And he could not even talk plain, but gobbled away in so thick a voice that no decent man could understand him, not that any wanted to.

It was the latter misfortune which attracted Saystrap's attention. A wizard's power lies in spells, and most of these must be chanted aloud in order to get the proper effect—even a short-time effect. An assistant who was as good as dumb, who would not learn a few tag ends of magic and then have the audacity to set up in business for himself, was the best to employ.

So one morning Saystrap arrived via a satisfactory puff of smoke in the middle of the cornfield where the landsman was berating his son for breaking a hoe. The smoke curled very impressively into the sky as Saystrap stepped out of its curtain. And the landsman jumped back a step or two, looking just as amazed as he should. Saystrap found this gratifying, a lucky omen, and prepared to bargain.

"Greetings," he said briskly. He had long ago learned that any long build-up was not for a short-spelled wizard. It was best to forgo the supposedly awed mumbles and get right to the point.

But he did not overlook the staging, of course. A pass or two in the air produced two apple trees, about shoulder height (he had to make it quick), still loaded with fruit. And, as an additional nice touch, a small dragon winked into existence and out again before the landsman found his voice. "It is a fair morning for field work," Saystrap continued.

"It was," the landsman returned uncertainly. Magic in the woods, or a cave now—that was one thing. But magic right out in the middle of the best yielding cornfield was a different matter. The dragon was gone, he could not really swear it had been here, but those trees were still standing where they would be a pesky nuisance around which to get the plow. "How— how can I serve you, Master—Master—?"

"Saystrap," supplied the wizard graciously. "I am your near neighbor, Master Ladizwell. Though busy as you have been on your very fruitful land you may not be aware of that."

Master Ladizwell looked from the trees to the wizard. There was a hint of a frown on his face. Wizards, like the lord's taxmen, were too apt to take more than they gave in return. He did not relish the thought of living cheek-by-jowl, as it were, with one. And he certainly had not invited this meeting.

"No, you have not," Saystrap answered his thought. This was the time to begin to bear down a little and let the fellow know just who and what he was dealing with. "I have come to ask your assistance in a small matter. I need a pair of younger feet, stronger arms, and a stout back to aid me. Now this lad"—for the first time he glanced at the younger son—"has he ever thought of going into service?"

"Him?" The landsman snorted. "Why, what fool would—" Then he stopped in mid-word. If this wizard did not know of his stupid son's uselessness, why tell the family shame abroad? "For what length of service?" he demanded quickly. If a long bond could be agreed upon he might get the lout out from underfoot, and make a profit into the bargain.

"Oh, the usual—a year and a day."

"And his wages, Master Saystrap?"

"How would you reckon his worth?"

"Well, now, at this season another pair of knowl-edgeable hands—" Ladizwell hurriedly kicked at the broken hoe, hoping the wizard had not seen that nor heard his hot words to his son.

"Will this suffice?" Saystrap waved a hand in a grand, wide gesture, and in the field stood a fine horse.

Ladizwell blinked. "Right enough!" he agreed hurriedly. He held out his hand and Saystrap slapped his into it, thus binding the bargain.

Then the wizard gestured again and smoke arose to wreathe both him and his newly engaged servant. When that cleared they had vanished and Ladizwell went to put a halter on the horse.

At dawn the next day, Ladizwell was far from pleased when he went to the stable to inspect his new prize and found a rabbit nibbling the straw in the stall but no horse. However, he thought, at least he did not have to feed and clothe that slip-fingered lout for a year and a day, so perhaps he was still better off than he had been yesterday.

Saystrap, back in his cave, was already making use of his new servant. To him this Joachim was a tool with neither wit nor will of his own. But the sooner he began to give what aid he could the better. Saystrap had to resolutely brush out of his mind visions of stone walls, treasure rooms, *things* pledged to his service; those were as heady as aged wine and not made to disturb working hours.

There were brews boiled and drunk—by Joachim. And he had to be led, or pushed and pulled, through patterns drawn in red and black on the rough floor. But in the end Saystrap was satisfied with the prelimi-

naries and went wearily to his hammock, leaving
Joachim to huddle on a bed of bracken.

At dawn the wizard was up and busy again. He
allowed Joachim a hasty—and to the lad very untasty—
meal of dried roots and berries, hurrying him until
Joachim was almost choking on the last begrudged
bite or two. Then they took to the traveling cloud
again and emerged from it not too far from the
Market Cross of Hill Dallow. That is—there strode
out of the cloud a man in a gray wool tunic leading a
fine frisky two-year-old colt, as promising an animal
as any one, lord or common, would want to lay eye
on. And this was sold at the first calling in the horse
fair for a bag of silver pieces heavy enough to weight
a man's belt in a satisfying manner.

The colt was led home by the buyer and shown off
as being an enviable bargain. But when the moon
rose, Joachim stole out of the barn, dropping stall
and door latch into place behind him. He shambled
off to the far side of the pasture where Saystrap
waited impatiently.

This was a game they played several times over,
always with a good gain thereby. Saystrap treated
Joachim well enough—though more as if he were
really a horse than any man. Which was Saystrap's
mistake. For Joachim might seem stupid, and be too
thick of speech to talk with his fellows, but he was
not correspondingly slow-witted. He learned from all
he heard and saw his master do. Deep in him a small
spark of ambition flared. There had not been anything about his father's land which had ever brought
that into being. For, no matter how hard he tried, his
brother, without seeming to put forth any great effort, could ably outdo him. But this was another
world than the farm.

Then, by chance, he learned something which even

Saystrap did not know, that spells were not always wedded to the spoken word.

His master had sent him to gather herbs for brews. This was wild country and men seldom traveled it. But furred and four-footed hunters had their own well-trodden trails.

For all the barrenness of the wild land Joachim was glad enough to be alone in the open. For, after what he now thought of as the homy comforts of the farmhouse (even with his father's caustic tongue, his brother's sneers to dim his days), he found the cave very damp and dreary, and he missed the fields more than he would have believed possible. It seemed a very long time since he had had a chance to lie and watch the slow passing of clouds overhead, dream of what he might do if he had a sorcerer's treasure now, or had been born into a lord's family.

But this day he found himself mulling over Saystrap's doings rather than paying attention to clouds, and his onetime dreams. In his mind he repeated the words he had heard the wizard use in spells. By now the change spell, at least, was as familiar to him as his own name. Then he heard a sound and looked around—into the yellow-green eyes of a snow cat. It hissed a challenge and Joachim knew that here stalked death on four paws. So, he concentrated—without being sure of how or on what.

The snow cat vanished! On the rock crouched a barn rat.

Joachim shivered. He put out his hand to test the reality of what he saw and the rat scuttled away squealing. Was this by any chance some ploy of Saystrap's, meant to frighten him into his work? But—there was another way of testing. Joachim looked down at his own body. Did he dare? He thought again.

Soft fur, paws with claws—he was a snow cat! Not quite believing, he leaped up, to bound along the ridge. Then he stopped beneath a rock spur, and thought himself a man again, more than a little frightened at his own act.

Then that fear became pride, the first time in his life he had cause to feel that. He was a wizard! But only in part. One spell alone could not make him a real one. He must learn more and more, and at the same time keep his secret from Saystrap if he could. Doubts about that gnawed him all the way back to the cave.

The only trouble was that Saystrap no longer tried other spells. And the few scraps Joachim assembled from his master's absent-minded mutterings were no help at all. Saystrap was concentrating on what he intended to be his greatest coup in shape-changing.

"The harvest fair at Garth Haigis is the chance to make a good profit," he told Joachim, mainly because he had to tell someone of his cleverness. "We must have something eye-catching to offer. A pity I cannot change you into a coffer of jewels. Then I could sell to more than one buyer. Only then, when the spell faded"—he laughed a little, evilly, and poked Joachim in the ribs with his staff-of-office—"you would be too widely scattered between one keep and the next ever to put you together again." He was deep in thought now, running his long forenail back and forth across his teeth.

"I wonder." He eyed Joachim appraisingly. "A cow is bait only for a landsman. And we have dealt too often in horses; there might be someone with a long memory there. Ah!" He tapped the end of his staff on the rock. "A trained hunting falcon—such brings a gleam of avarice to any lord's eye!"

Joachim was uneasy. True enough, Saystrap's trick

had always worked smoothly. He had had no trouble freeing himself from barns and stables when the spell lifted. But keeps were better guarded and it might not be easy to flee out of those. Then he thought of his own secret. He might, in the allotted time, cease to be Saystrap's falcon, but that did not mean he had to become an easily recognized man.

The fair at Garth Haigis was an important one. Joachim, wearing falcon shape, gazed about eagerly from his perch on Saystrap's saddle horn. Men in booths remarked on the fine bird and asked its price. But the wizard set such a high one, they all shook their heads, though one or two went so far as to count the silver in their belt purses.

Before noon a man wearing the Cross-Key badge of Lord Tanheff rode up to Saystrap.

"A fine bird that, fit for a lord's mews. My lord would like to look at it, Master Falconer."

So Saystrap rode behind the servant to the upper field where tents were set up for the comfort of the nobly born. There they summoned to them merchants with such wares as they found interesting.

Lord Tanheff was a man of middle years and he had no son to lift shield after him. But his daughter, the Lady Juluya, sat at his right hand. Since she was a great heiress she had a goodly gathering of young lords, each striving to win her attention. It was her way to be fair and show no one favor over his fellows.

She was small and thin, and had she not been an heiress none perhaps would have found her a beauty. But she had a smile which could warm a man's heart (even if he forgot the gold and lands behind it), and eyes which were interested in all they saw. Once Joachim looked upon her he could not see anything else.

Neither could Saystrap. It suddenly flashed into his mind as a great illuminating truth that there were other ways of gaining a keep than through difficult spells. One such way was marriage. He did not doubt that, could he gain access to the lady, he would win her. Was he not a wizard and so master of such subtleties that these clods sighing around her now could not imagine?

His planned trickery might also be turned to account. For if he sold Joachim to her father, and the bird apparently escaped and returned to him, then he could enter the lady's own hall to bring it back, and with him would be other tricks. He could use the pretense of the strayed bird to open all doors.

"Father—that falcon! It is a lordly bird," the Lady Juluya cried as she saw Joachim.

He felt the warmth of pride. Though she saw him as a bird, he was admired. Then he lost that pride. Let her see him as he really was and she would speedily turn away.

Lord Tanheff was as pleased as his daughter and quickly struck a bargain with Saystrap. But the wizard whispered into the bird's ear before he placed it on the gloved hand of the lord's falconer:

"Return swiftly tonight!"

Joachim, still watching the Lady Juluya, did not really heed that order. For he was wondering why, at the moment of change, he could not wish himself into some guise which would bring him close to the lady. However, he did not have long to watch her, for the falconer took him to the keep. Joachim stood on a perch in the mews, hooded now and seeing nothing, left in the dark to get the feel of his new home as was the way with a bird in a strange place. He could hear other hawks moving restlessly, and, beyond, the noises of the keep. He wondered how

Saystrap thought he could get out of this place in man's shape. Had the wizard some magic plan ready to cover that?

Joachim guessed right there. The wizard knew that his falcon-turned-man could not leave the mews as easily as a landsman's barn. He did not trust his assistant to have wits enough to work out any reasonable escape. He himself would move cautiously to effect Joachim's release and not allow magic to be suspected, not when he planned to enchant the Lady Juluya. So Saystrap sat down in a copse near the keep to await moonrise.

At sunset, however, the clouds gathered and it was plain that no moon would show. Saystrap could not summon moon magic now, but perhaps he could put the coming storm to account. If he could only be sure when Joachim's change would occur, a matter with which he had never concerned himself before. Had it not been for his new plan to win the Lady Juluya, the wizard would not have cared what happened to Joachim. Stupid lads could always be found, but a wizard was entitled to keep his own skin safe. Lord Tanheff, if he did suspect spells, would be just the sort to appeal to a major sorcerer for protection. Saystrap, for all his self-esteem, was not blinded to his own peril from an encounter of that kind.

He could not sit still, but paced back and forth, trying to measure time. To be too early would be as fatal as being too late. The cloud-traveling spell could not be held long, and if Joachim could not take to its cover at once, Saystrap could not summon it again that night. He bit his thumbnail, cursing the rain now beginning to fall.

At the keep that same rain drove men to take cover indoors. Joachim heard footsteps in the mews, the voices of the falconer and his assistant. His time for change was close. He shifted on the perch and the bells fastened to his jesses rang. The footsteps were closing in and—the change was now!

Suddenly he was standing on his own two feet, blinking into the light of a lantern the falconer held. The man's mouth opened for a shout of alarm. Joachim thought his mind spell.

A snow cat crouched snarling, and the falconer, with some presence of mind, threw his lantern at that fearsome beast before he took to his heels, Joachim in great bounds behind. But, as the shouting falconer broke one way out of the door, Joachim streaked in the other, trying to reach the outer wall.

That was far too high to leap over, but he sped up the stairs leading to the narrow defense walk along its top. Men shouted, a torch was thrown, nearly striking him. Joachim leaped at a guard aiming a spear, knocked the man down, and was over him and on. But ahead more men were gathering, bending bows. He thought—

There was no cat on the wall—nothing! The men-at-arms hurried forward, thudding spear heads into every patch of shadow, unable to believe that the animal had vanished.

"Wizardry! Tell my lord quickly. There is wizardry here!"

Some stayed to patrol by twos and threes, no man wanting to walk alone in the dark with wizardry loose. The storm struck harder, water rushed over the wall. It washed with such force that it swept away a small gold ring no man had seen in that dusk, carrying it along a gutter, tumbling it out and down, to fall to the muddy earth of the inner garden where the Lady Juluya and her maids grew sweet herbs and flowers. There it lay under the drooping branches of a rain-heavy rose bush.

When the Lord Tanheff heard the report of the falconer and the wall guards, he agreed that it was plain the falcon had been enchanted, and this was some stroke of wizardry aimed at the keep. He then dispatched one of his heralds to ride night and day to demand help from the nearest reputable sorcerer, one to whom he had already paid a retaining fee as insurance against just such happenings. In the meantime he cautioned all to keep within the walls; the gates were not to be opened for any cause until the herald returned.

Saystrap heard the morning rumors at the fair where men now looked suspiciously at their neighbors, bundling their goods away to be on the road again, though the fair was not officially over. With magic loose who knew where it would strike next? Better be safe, if flatter of purse. The lord had sent for a sorcerer—with magic opposed to magic anything might happen to innocent bystanders. Magic was no respecter of persons.

However, the wizard did not give up his plan for the Lady Juluya, it was such a good one. Common sense did not even now baffle his hopes. So he lurked in hiding and made this new plan and that, only to be forced to discard each after some study.

The Lady Juluya, walking in her scrap of garden, stooped to raise a rain-soaked rose and saw a glint in the mud. Curious, she dug, to uncover a ring which seemed to slip on her finger almost of its own accord.

"Wherever did you come from?" She held her hand into the watery sunshine of the morning, admiring the ring, more than a little pleased at her luck in finding it. Since all her maids denied its loss she finally decided that it must have lain buried for years until the heavy rain washed it free, and she could claim it for her own.

Two days passed, three, and still the herald did not return. The Lord Tanheff did not permit the keep gates to be opened. The fairground was deserted now. Saystrap, driven to a rough hiding place in the woods, gnawed his nails down to the quick. Only a fanatical stubbornness kept him lurking there.

None in the lady's tower knew that when she took to her bed at night the ring grew loose and slipped from her finger, to become a mouse feasting on crumbs from her table. Joachim realized that this was a highly dangerous game he played. It would be much wiser to assume wings and feathers once more and be out of the castle with three or four good flaps of his wings. Yet he could not bring himself to leave.

The Lady Juluya was courted and flattered much, yet she was a girl of wit and good humor, wise enough to keep her head. She was both kind and courteous. Time and time again Joachim was tempted to take his true form and tell her his story. But she was seldom alone, and when she was he could not bring himself to do it. Who was he—a loutish clod, so stupid and clumsy he could not even work in the fields nor speak plainly. At his mere appearance he was sure she would summon a guard immediately. And talk!—he could not tell them anything so they would understand.

After the first night he did not remain a mouse, but went out onto the balcony and became a man, squatting in the deepest pool of shadow. He thought about speech, and how hard it was for him to shape words to sound like those of others. So he practiced saying in whispers the strange sounds he had heard Saystrap mumble, tongue twisters though they were. He did not use them for the binding of spells, but merely to listen to his own voice. By daybreak he was certain, to his great joy, that he did speak more clearly than he ever had before.

In the scrap of wood Saystrap had at last fastened upon a plan he thought would get him into the keep. If he could then be private with the lady only for a short space, he was certain he could bind her to his will and all would be as he wished. He had seen the herald ride forth and knew that it might not be too long before he would return with aid.

Though the gates were shut, birds flew over the wall. And piegeons made their nests in the towers and along the roofs. On the fourth day Saystrap assumed a feathered form to join them.

They wheeled and circled, cooed, fluttered, peered in windows, preened on balconies and windowsills. In her garden the Lady Juluya shook out grain for them and Saystrap was quick to take advantage of such a summons, coming to earth before her.

There is this about wizardry: if you have dabbled even the nail tip of one finger in it, then you have gained knowledge beyond that of ordinary men. That ring which was Joachim recognized the pigeon that was Saystrap. At first he thought his master had come seeking him. Then he noted the wizard-pigeon ran a little this way, back that, and so was pacing out a spell pattern about the feet of the Lady Juluya.

Joachim did not know what would happen if Saystrap completed that magic, but he feared the worst. So he loosed his grip on the lady's finger and spun out, to land across one of the lines the pigeon's feet were marking so exactly.

Saystrap looked at the ring and knew it. He wanted none of Joachim, though he was shaken at meeting his stupid apprentice in such a guise. However, one thing at a time, and if this spell was now spoiled or hindered he might not have another chance. He could

settle with Joachim later, after his purpose was accomplished. So, with a sharp peck of bill, he sent the
ring flying.

Joachim spun behind the rose bush. Then he crept
forth again, this time a velvet-footed tom cat. He
pounced, and the wildly fluttering piegon was between his jaws.

"Drop it—you cruel thing!" Lady Juluya struck at
the cat. But, still gripping the pigeon, Joachim dodged
and ran into the courtyard.

Then he found he held no pigeon, but a snarling
dog twice his size broke from his grip. He leaped
away from Saystrap to the top of a barrel and there
grew wings, beak, and talons, once more a falcon,
able to soar about the leaping, slavering hound so
eager to reach him.

There was no dog, but a thing straight out of a
nightmare, half scaled, with leathery wings more
powerful than Joachim's, and a lashing tail with a
wicked spiked end. The creature spiraled up after the
falcon into the sky.

He could perhaps outfly it if he headed for the
open country. But he sensed that Saystrap was not
intent upon herding an unwilling apprentice back to
servitude. He was after the Lady Juluya, therefore
there must be fight not flight.

From the monster came such a force of gathered
power that Joachim weakened. His poor feat of wizardry was feeble opposed to Saystrap's. With a last
despairing beat of wings, he landed on the roof of
Lady Juluya's tower and found himself sliding down
it, once more a man. While above him circled the
griffon, seeming well content to let him fall to his
death on the pavement below.

Joachim summoned power for one last thought.

He fell through the air a gray pebble. So small and

dark a thing escaped Saystrap's eyes. The pebble struck the pavement and rolled into a crack.

Saystrap meanwhile turned to bring victory out of defeat. He alighted in the courtyard and seized upon the Lady Juluya to bear her away. The pebble rolled from hiding and Joachim stood there. Bare-handed, he threw himself at the monster. This time he shouted words clear and loud, the counterspell which returned Saystrap to his own proper form. Grappling with the wizard, he bore him to the ground, trying to gag him with one hand over his mouth that he might not utter any more spells.

At that moment the herald rode in upon them as they struggled, ringed around (at a safe distance) by the keep folk who were not afraid to be caught in the backlash of any spells from the tangle.

Lord Tanheff shouted an order from the door of the hall to where he had swept his daughter. The herald tossed at the fighters the contents of a box he had brought back with him (price: one ruby, two medium-sized topazes). There was a burst of light, a clap of thunder, and Joachim stumbled out of a puff of smoke groping his way blindy. A fat black spider sped in the opposite direction, only to be gobbled up by a rooster.

Well pleased now that they had someone reasonably normal in appearance to blame for all the commotion, the men-at-arms seized Joachim. When he tried to use his spell he found it did not work. Then the Lady Juluya called imperiously:

"Let him alone!" she ordered. "It was he who attacked the monster on my behalf. Let him tell us who and what he is—"

Let him tell, thought Joachim in despair, *but I cannot do that*. He looked dejectedly at the Lady Juluya watching him so eagerly, and knew that he must at least try. As he ran his tongue over his lips she prompted him encouragingly:

"Tell us first who you are."

"Joachim," he croaked miserably.

"You are a wizard?"

He shook his head. "Never more than a very small part of one, my lady." So eager was he to let her know the truth of it all, that he forgot his stumbling tongue, all else but the tale he had to tell. He told it in a flow of words all could understand.

When he was done, she clapped her hands together and cried: "A fine, brave tale. I claim you equal to such acts. Wizard, half-wizard, third or fourth part of a wizard that you may be, you are surely a man to be reckoned with, Joachim. I would like to know you better."

He smiled a little timidly. But inwardly he vowed, though he might be finished with wizardry, any one the Lady Juluya claimed to be a man had a right to pride. Fortune had served him well this time. If he meddled in magic concerns again it might not continue to do so.

In that he was a wise man—as he later had chance to prove on numerous occasions. Joachim, his foot firmly planted on the road to success in that hour, never turned back nor faltered.

But the rooster had a severe pain in its middle and was forced to disgorge the spider. How damaged it was by that abrupt meeting with the irony of Fate no man knew thereafter, for Saystrap disappeared.

Legacy From Sorn Fen

By the western wall of Klavenport on the Sea of Autumn Mists—but you do not want a bard's beginning to my tale, Goodmen? Well enough, I have no speak-harp to twang at all the proper times. And this is not altogether a tale for lords-in-their-halls. Though the beginning did lie in Klavenport right enough.

It began with one Higbold. It was after the Invaders' War and those were times when small men, if they had their wits sharpened, could rise in the world—swiftly, if fortune favored them. Which is a bard's way of saying they knew when to use the knife point, when to swear falsely, when to put hands on what was not rightfully theirs.

Higbold had his rats running to his whistle, and then his hounds to his horn. Finally no one spoke (save behind a shielding hand, glancing now and then over his shoulder) about his beginnings. He settled in the Gate Keep of Klavenport, took command there, married a wife who was hall-born (there were such to be given to landless and shieldless men then, their

193

kin so harried by war, or dead in it, that they went gladly to any one who offered a roof over their heads, meat in the dish, and mead in the cup before them). Higbold's lady was no more nor less than her sisters in following expediency.

Save that from the harsh days before her marriage she held memories. Perhaps it was those which made her face down Higbold himself in offering charity to those begging from door to door.

Among those came Caleb. He lacked an eye and walked with a lurch which nigh spilled him sprawling every time he took a full stride. What age he was no one could say; cruel mauling puts years on a man.

It might have been that the Lady Isbel knew him from the old days, but if so neither spoke of that. He became one of the household, working mainly in the small walled garden. They say that he was one with the power of growing things, that herbs stood straight and sweet-smelling for him, flowers bloomed richly under his tending.

Higbold had nothing to interest him in the garden. Save that now and then he met someone there where they could stand well in the open, walls too often having ears. For Higbold's ambition did not end in the keepership of the Kalvenport Gate. Ah, no, such a man's ambition never ceases to grow. But you can gain only so much by showing a doubled fist, or a bared sword. After a certain point you must accomplish your means more subtly, by influencing men's minds, not the enslavement of their bodies. Higbold studied well.

What was said and done in the garden one night in early midsummer was never known. But Higbold had a witness he did not learn about until too late. Only servants gossip as always about their masters, and there is a rumor that Caleb went to the Lady Isbel to talk privately. Then he took his small bundle of worldly goods and went forth, not only from the gate keep, but out of Klavenport as well, heading west on the highway.

Near the port there had been repairing, rebuilding, and the marks of the Invaders' War had faded from the land. But Caleb did not keep long to the highway. He was a prudent man, and knew that roads made for swift travel can lead hunters on a man's tracks.

Cross-country was hard, doubly so for his twisted body. He came to the fringes of the Fen of Sorn. Ah, I see you shake your heads and draw faces at that! Rightly do you so, Goodmen, rightly. We all know that there are parts of High Hallack which belong to the Old Ones, where men with sense in their thick skulls do not walk.

But it was there Caleb found that others had been before him. They were herdsmen who had been driving the wild hill cattle (those which ranged free during the war) to market. Something had frightened the beasts and sent them running. Now the herders, half-mad with the thought of losing all reward of their hard labor, tracked them into the fen.

However, in so doing, they came upon something else. No, I shall not try to describe what they started out of its lair. You all know that there are secrets upon secrets in places like the fen. Enough to say that this had the appearance of a woman, enough to incite the lust of the drovers who had been kept long from the lifting of any skirt. Having cornered the creature, they were having their sport.

Caleb had not left Klavenport unarmed. In spite of his twisted body he was an expert with crossbow. Now he again proved his skill. Twice he fired and men howled like beasts—or worse than beasts seeing what they had been doing—beasts do not so use their females.

Caleb shouted as if he were leading a group of men-at-arms. The herders floundered away. Then he went down to what they had left broken behind them.

No man knows what happened thereafter, for Caleb spoke of it to no one. But in time he went on alone, though his face was white and his work-hardened hands shook.

He did not venture into the fen, but traveled, almost as one with a set purpose, along its edge. Two nights did he camp so. What he did and with whom he spoke, why those came—who can tell? But on the morning of the third day he turned his back on Sorn Fen and started toward the highway.

It was odd but as he walked his lurching skip-step was not so evident, as if, with every stride he took, his twisted body seemed straighter. By the night of the fourth day he walked near as well as any man who was tired and footsore might. It was then that he came to the burned-out shell of the Inn at the Forks.

Once that had been a prosperous house. Much silver had spun across its tables into the hands of the keeper and his family. It was built at a spot where two roads, one angling north, one south, met, to continue thereon into Klavenport. But the day of its glory passed before the Battle of Falcon Cut. For five winter seasons or more its charred timbers had been a dismal monument to the ravages of war, offering no cheer for the traveler.

Now Caleb stood looking at its sad state and—

Believe this or not as you will, Goodmen. But suddenly here was no burned-out ruin. Rather stood an inn. Caleb, showing no surprise, crossed the road to enter. Enter it as master, for as such he was hailed by those about their business within its courtyard.

Now there were more travelers up and down the
western roads, for this was the season of trade with
Klavenport. So it was not long before the tale of the
restored inn reached the city. There were those unable to believe such a report, who rode out, curious,
to prove it true.

They found it much as the earlier inn had been.
Though those who had known it before the war
claimed there were certain differences. However, when
they were challenged to name these, they were vague.
But all united in the information that Caleb was host
there and that he had changed with the coming of
prosperity, for prosperous he certainly now was.

Higbold heard those reports. He did not frown, but
he rubbed his forefinger back and forth under his
thick lower lip. Which was a habit of his when he
thought deeply, considering this point and that. Then
he summoned to him a flaunty, saucy piece in skirts.
She had long thrown herself in his direction when-
ever she could. It was common knowledge that, while
Higbold had indeed bedded his lady in the early days
of their marriage, to make sure that none could break
the tie binding them, he was no longer to be found in
her chamber, taking his pleasures elsewhere. Though
as yet with none under his own roof.

Now he spoke privately with Elfra, and set in her
hands a slip of parchment. Then openly he berated
her loudly, had her bustled roughly, thrown into the
street without so much as a cloak about her shoulders. She wept and wailed, and took off along the
western road.

In time she reached the Inn at the Forks. Her
journey had not been an easy one so she crept into
the courtyard as much a beggar in looks as any of the
stinking, shuffling crowd who hung around a merchant's door in the city. Save that when she spoke to

Caleb she gave him a bit of parchment with on it a
message which might have been writ in my lady's
hand. Caleb welcomed her and at length he made her
waiting maid in the tap room. She did briskly well,
such employment suiting her nature.

The days passed. Time slid from summer into
autumn. At length the Ice Dragon sent his frost breath
over the land. It was then that Elfra stole away with a
merchant bound for Klavenport. Caleb, hearing of
her going, shrugged and said that if she thought so to
better her life the choice was hers.

But Elfra stayed with the merchant only long enough
to reach the gate. From there she went directly to
Higbold's own chamber. At first, as he listened, there
was that in his face which was not good to see. But
she did not take warning, sure that he looked so only
because her tale was so wild. To prove the truth of
her words she held her hand over the table.

About her thumb (so large it was that she could
not wear it elsewhere on her woman's hand) was a
ring of green stone curiously patterned with faint red
lines as if veined with blood. Holding it directly in
Higbold's sight, Elfra made a wish.

Below on the table there appeared a necklace of
gems, such a necklace as might well be the ransom
for a whole city in the days of the war. Higbold
sucked in his breath, his face gone blank, his eyes
half hooded by their lids.

Then his hand shot out and imprisoned her wrist in
a grim grip and he had off that ring. She looked into
his face and began to whimper, learning too late that
she was only a tool, and one which had served its
purpose now, and having served its purpose—

She was gone!

But Higbold cupped the ring between his palms
and smiled evilly.

Shortly thereafter at the Inn flames burst out. No man could fight their fierce heat as they ate away what the magic of the Old Ones had brought into being. Once more Caleb stood in the cold owning nothing. Nothing, that is, except his iron will.

He wasted no time in regrets, nor in bewailing that lack of caution which had lost him his treasure. Rather he turned and began to stride along the road. When he came to a certain place he cut away from the path of men. Though snow blew about him, and a knife-edged wind cut like a lash at his back, he headed for the fen.

Again time passed. No one rebuilt, by magic or otherwise, the Inn. But with Higbold things happened. Those who had once been firm against him became his supporters, or else suffered various kinds of chastening misfortune. His lady kept to her chamber. It was rumored that she ailed and perhaps would not live out the year.

There had never been a king of High Hallack, for the great lords held themselves all equal, one to another. None would have given support to a fellow to set him over the rest. But Higbold was not of their company, and so it might be a matter of either unite against him, or acknowledge his rulership. Still those men expected to be foremost in opposition to his rise seemed oddly hesitant to take any step to prevent it.

In the meantime there were rumors concerning a man who lived on the fringe of Sorn Fen and who was a tamer of beasts, even a seller of them. A merchant, enterprising and on the search for something unique, was enough intrigued by such tales to make a detour. He came into Klavenport from that side venture with three strange animals.

They were small, yet they had the look of the fierce snow cats of the high range. Only these were obviously tame, so tame that they quickly enchanted the merchants' wives and the ladies of the city into wanting them for pets. Twice the merchant returned to the fen fringe and bought more of the cats—well pleased each time with his bargain.

Then he needed an export permit and had to go to Higbold. So he came to the Keep bringing a "sweetener" for dealing after the custom—that being one of the cats. Higbold was not one with a liking for animals. His horses were tools to be used, and no hound ever lay in his hall or chamber. But he had the cat carried on to his lady's bower. Perhaps he thought that he would not have to consider her for long and this gift might give some coating of pretense.

Shortly after, he began to dream. Now there was certainly enough in his past to provide ill dreams for not one man but a troop. However, it was not of the past that he dreamed, but rather of the present, and perhaps a dark future. For in each of these dreams (and they were real enough to bring him starting up in bed calling for candles as he woke out of them), he had lost the ring Elfra had brought him—the ring now the core of all his schemes.

He had worn it secretly on a cord around his neck under his clothing. However, all his dreams were of it slipping from that security. So now when he slept he grasped it within his hand.

Then one morning he awoke to find it gone. Fear rode him hard until he found it among the covers on his bed. At last his night terrors drove him to putting it under his tongue as he slept. His tempers were such that those in close contact with him went in fear of their lives.

At last came the night when he dreamed again and this time the dream seemed very real. Something crouched first at the foot of his bed, and then it began a slow, slinking advance, stalking up the length of it. He could not move, but had to lie sweating, awaiting its coming.

Suddenly he roused out of that nightmare, sneezing. The ring lay where he had coughed it forth. By it crouched the strange cat, its eyes glowing so that he would swear it was no cat, but something else, more intelligent and malignant, which had poured its being into the cat's small body. It watched him with cold measurement and he was frozen, unable to put forth his hand to the ring. Then, calmly, it took up that circlet of green and red in its mouth, leaped from the bed and was gone.

Higbold cried out and grabbed. But the creature was already at the door of the chamber, streaking through as the guard came in answer to his lord's call. Higbold thrust the man aside as he raced to follow.

"The cat!" His shouts alarmed the whole keep. "Where is the cat?"

But it was the hour before daybreak when men were asleep. Those aroused by his shouting blinked and were amazed for a moment or two.

Higbold well knew that there were a hundred, no, a thousand places within that pile where such a small animal might hide, or drop to eternal loss that which it carried. That thought created frenzy in his brain, so that at first he was like one mad, racing to and fro, shouting to watch, to catch the cat.

Then came a messenger from the gate saying that the cat had been seen to leap the wall and run from the Keep, and the city, out into the country. Deep in him Higbold knew a growing cold which was like the chill of death, since it heralded the end of all his plans. For if the Keep provided such a wealth of hiding places, then what of the countryside?

He returned, stricken silent now with the fullness of his loss, to his chamber. There he battered his bare fists against the stone of the wall, until the pain of his self-bruising broke through the torment in his mind and he could think clearly again.

Animals could be hunted. He had hounds in his kennels, though he had never wasted time in the forms of the chase in which the high-born delighted. He would hunt that cat as no beast in High Hallack had ever been hunted before. Having come to his senses, he gave orders in a tone of voice that made those about him flinch and look sidewise, keeping as distant as they dared.

In the hour before dawn the hunt was up, though it was a small party riding out of the Keep. Higbold had ordered with him only the master of hounds with a brace of the best trail keepers, and his squire.

The trail was so fresh and clear the hounds ran eagerly. But they did not pad along the highway, taking at once to open ground. This speedily grew more difficult for the riders, until the dogs far outstripped the men. Only their belling voices, raised now and then, told those laboring after that they still held the track. Higbold now had his fear under tight control, he did not push his horse, but there was a tenseness in the lines of his body which suggested that, if he could have grown wings, he would have soared ahead in an instant.

Wilder and rougher grew the country. The laboring squire's horse was lamed and had to drop behind. Higbold did not even spare him a glance. The sun was up and ahead was that smooth green of the fen country. In Higbold that frozen cold was nigh his heart. If the fleeing cat took into that there would be no following.

When they reached the outer fringe of that dire

land the trail turned at an angle and ran along the edge, as if the creature had willfully decided not to trust to the promised safety beyond.

At length they came upon a small hut, built of the very material of this forsaken land, boulders and stones set together for its walls, a thatch of rough branches for roof. As they approached the hounds were suddenly thrown back as if they had run into an invisible wall. They yapped and leaped, and were again hurled to earth, their clamor wild.

Their master dismounted from his blowing horse and ran forward. Then he, too, met resistance. He stumbled and almost fell, putting out his hands and running them from right to left. He might have been stroking some surface.

Higbold came out of the saddle and strode forward. "What is it?" For the first time in hours he spoke, his words grating on the ear.

"There—there is a wall, Lord—" quavered the master, and he shrank back from both the place and Higbold.

Higbold continued to tramp on. He passed the master and the slavering, whining hounds. The man, the dogs, were mad. There was no wall, there was only the hut and what he sought in it.

He set hand on the warped surface of the door and slammed it open with the full force of his frustration.

Before him was a rough table, a stool. On the stool sat Caleb. On the table top crouched the cat, purring under the measured stroking of the man's gentle hand. By the animal lay the ring.

Higbold stove to put out his hand, to snatch up that treasure. From the moment he sighted it, that had his full attention. The animal, the man, meant nothing to him. But now Caleb's other hand dropped loosely over the circlet. Higbold was powerless to move.

"Higbold," Caleb addressed him directly, using no polite forms or title, "you are an evil man, but one of power—too much power. In the past year you have used that very cleverly. A crown is nigh within your grasp—is that not so?"

Soft and smooth he spoke as one entirely without fear. He had no weapon, only lounged at his ease. Higbold's hatred now outweighed his fear, so that he wanted nothing so much as to smash the other's face into crimson ruin. Yet he could not stir so much as a finger.

"You have, I think," Caleb continued, "greatly enjoyed your possession of this." He raised his hand a little to show the ring.

"Mine—!" Higbold's throat hurt as he shaped that thick word.

"No." Caleb shook his head, still gently, as one might to a child who demanded what was not and never could be his. "I shall tell you a tale, Higbold. This ring was a gift, freely given to me. I was able to ease somewhat the dying of one who was not of our kind, but had been death-dealt by those like you in spirit. Had she not been taken unawares she would have had her defenses, defenses such as you now taste. But she was tricked, and then used with such cruelty as would shame any one daring to call himself one of us. Because I tried to aid, though there was little I could do, I was left this token—and my keeping it was confirmed by her people. It can only be used for a limited time, however. I intended to use it for good. That is a thought to make you smile, isn't it, Higbold?

"Then you used your lady's name to beg of me aid for one I thought badly treated. So, in my blindness, I brought about my own betrayal. I am a simple man, but there are things even the simple can do. To have

Higbold for High King over this land—that is wrong—
beyond one's own wishes or fears.

"So I spoke again to those of the fen, and with
their aid I set a trap—to bring you hither. And you
came, easily enough. Now." He lifted his hand and
let the ring lie. It seemed there was a glow about it
and again Higbold's eyes were drawn to it and he
saw nothing else. Out of sight, beyond the gleaming
green and red of the ring, a voice spoke.

"Take up the ring you wish so much, Higbold. Set
it on your finger once again. Then go and claim your
kingdom!"

Higbold found that now he could stretch forth his
hand. His fingers closed about the ring. Hurriedly,
lest it be rift from him once more, he pushed it on his
finger.

He did not look again at Caleb, instead he turned
and went out of the hut, as if the other man had
ceased to exist. The hounds lay on their muddied
bellies, whimpering a little as they licked at paws
sore from their long run. Their master squatted on his
heels watching for his lord's return. Their two horses
stood with drooping heads, foam roping their bits.

Higbold did not move toward his mount, nor did
he speak to the waiting hound master. Instead he
faced west and south a little. As one who marches
toward a visible and long desired goal, paying no
heed to that about him, he strode toward the fen. His
hound master did not move to stop him. Staring
drop-jawed, he watched him go, until he was swallowed up in the mists.

Caleb came forth from the hut, the cat riding on
his shoulder, and stood at ease. It was he who broke
silence first.

"Return to your lady, my friend, and say to her

that Higbold has gone to seek his kingdom. He shall not return.''

Then he, also, went to where the mists of the fen wreathed him around and he could no longer be seen.

When the master came again to Klavenport he told the Lady Isbel what he had seen and heard. Thereafter, she seemed to gather strength (as if some poison drained or shadow lifted from her) and came forth from her chamber. She set about making arrangements to give gifts from the wealth of Higbold.

When summer reached its height she rode forth before dawn, taking only one waiting maid (one who had come with her from her father's house and was tied with long bonds of loyalty). They were seen to follow the highway for a space as the guards watched. Thereafter no man marked where they went, and they were not seen again.

Whether she went to seek her lord, or another, who knows? For the Fen of Sorn renders not to our blood its many secrets.

DAW

The really great fantasy books are published by DAW:

Andre Norton

☐ LORE OF THE WITCH WORLD   UE2012—$3.50
☐ HORN CROWN   UE1635—$2.95
☐ PERILOUS DREAMS   UE1749—$2.50

C.J. Cherryh

☐ THE DREAMSTONE   UE2013—$3.50
☐ THE TREE OF SWORDS AND JEWELS   UE1850—$2.95

Lin Carter

☐ DOWN TO A SUNLESS SEA   UE1937—$2.50
☐ DRAGONROUGE   UE1982—$2.50

M.A.R. Barker

☐ THE MAN OF GOLD   UE1940—$3.95

Michael Shea

☐ NIFFT THE LEAN   UE1783—$2.95
☐ THE COLOR OUT OF TIME   UE1954—$2.50

B.W. Clough

☐ THE CRYSTAL CROWN   UE1922—$2.75

NEW AMERICAN LIBRARY
P.O. Box 999, Bergenfield, New Jersey 07621

Please send me the DAW Books I have checked above. I am enclosing
$_____ (check or money order—no currency or C.O.D.'s).
Please include the list price plus $1.00 per order to cover handling
costs.

Name _____

Address _____

City _____ State _____ Zip Code _____
Please allow at least 4 weeks for delivery

DAW

DAW BRINGS YOU THESE BESTSELLERS BY MARION ZIMMER BRADLEY

- ☐ DARKOVER LANDFALL   UE1906—$2.50
- ☐ THE SPELL SWORD   UE1891—$2.25
- ☐ THE HERITAGE OF HASTUR   UE1967—$3.50
- ☐ THE SHATTERED CHAIN   UE1961—$3.50
- ☐ THE FORBIDDEN TOWER   UE2029—$3.95
- ☐ TWO TO CONQUER   UE1876—$2.95
- ☐ SHARRA'S EXILE   UE1988—$3.95
- ☐ HAWKMISTRESS!   UE1958—$3.50
- ☐ THENDARA HOUSE   UE1857—$3.50
- ☐ CITY OF SORCERY   UE1962—$3.50

- ☐ HUNTERS OF THE RED MOON   UE1968—$2.50
- ☐ THE SURVIVORS   UE1861—$2.95

Anthologies

- ☐ THE KEEPER'S PRICE   UE1931—$2.50
- ☐ SWORD OF CHAOS   UE1722—$2.95
- ☐ SWORD AND SORCERESS   UE1928—$2.95

NEW AMERICAN LIBRARY
P.O. Box 999, Bergenfield, New Jersey 07621

Please send me the DAW Books I have checked above. I am enclosing
$_____ (check or money order—no currency or C.O.D.'s).
Please include the list price plus $1.00 per order to cover handling
costs.

Name _____

Address _____

City _____ State _____ Zip Code _____

Allow 4-6 weeks for delivery